Sherlock Holmes and The Tomb of Terror

By the same author

Sherlock Holmes and the Egyptian Hall Adventure
Sherlock Holmes and the Eminent Thespian
Sherlock Holmes and the Brighton Pavilion Mystery
Sherlock Holmes and the Houdini Birthright
Sherlock Holmes and the Man Who Lost Himself
Sherlock Holmes and the Greyfriars School Mystery
Sherlock Holmes and the Yule-tide Mystery
Sherlock Holmes and the Theatre of Death
Sherlock Holmes and the Baker Street Dozen
Sherlock Holmes and the Circus of Fear
Sherlock Holmes and the Sandringham House Mystery

Sherlock Holmes
and
The Tomb of Terror

Val Andrews

BREESE
BOOKS
LONDON

First published in 2000 by
Breese Books Ltd
164 Kensington Park Road, London W11 2ER, England

ISBN: 0 947 533 72 9

Typeset in 11½/14pt Caslon by
Ann Buchan (Typesetters), Middlesex
Printed and bound in Great Britain by
Itchen Printers Ltd, Southampton

PREFACE
by
Colonel George Court, FZS

Perhaps at this point the decent thing for me to do is introduce myself: my name is George Court and I am not only an explorer (it was I who discovered that the reticulated Nile Crocodile is an entirely new species which scientists had long mistaken for a sub-species), but a book collector with a great interest in crime and detective fiction of the classic variety. Since my retirement from the army I have spent a good deal of my time browsing in secondhand book shops and stalls where one can sometimes pick up the odd bargain. Northerners (and cracking good chaps they are too) have an expression: 'Where there is muck there is brass!' Any book collector will back up this quaint saying, for where the books have been lovingly sorted and smartened up the prices are high.

With all this in mind I was sorting through a pile of extremely well-worn volumes, roughly heaped next to a stall in a side street in Islington, when I came across a book that interested me, a copy of the *African Diaries* of H.M. Stanley. It was neither rare nor was it in very good condition, but I reckoned it would sit well upon my shelf of such tomes and the price pencilled inside was a mere sixpence. So I picked it up and held it aloft, giving the man behind the stall a sixpence. He grunted in the way of such persons and I wandered upon my business with the book under my arm. It was not until I had reached a Lyons' Teashop and seated myself at a familiar marble-topped table that I was able to examine my purchase more fully. The volume was a little more dilapidated than I had at first thought with a sad excuse for a binding, but as the cockney fellows would say: 'Wotcha expec' fer a tanner?' (Cracking good chaps though, by the way!) Having checked that all the plates were intact I turned to the title page. Glancing at this I noticed a name, written clearly inside the front cover: 'John H. Watson': evidently an earlier owner of the book. Of course as a disciple of the great Sherlock Holmes, his Boswell's name instantly rang bells in my head, but then, I mused, there must be a fifty thousand Watsons in London alone, and possibly several thousand John Watsons, aye and perhaps a hundred or two John H. Watsons.

Then it fell from between the leaves of the volume: 'it' being a double sheet of foolscap, closely pen written. My heart beat a little faster as I caught words like 'Holmes' and 'Baker Street' at a mere glance. A closer inspection revealed that it was a form of synopsis for an as yet unpublished Sherlock Holmes novel! My hands must have shaken as I opened up the folio and quickly read each word. Was it genuine, and had the good doctor actually sat burning the midnight oil and guiding his Waverley across the page?

The average owner of the secondhand book shop or stall is cast from a rough mould as far as his temper is concerned. I have dealt with many in my time and have yet to find one who had a friendly or even icily polite manner. I imagine that dealing with collectors and browsers has something to do with it. Many might be termed as time wasters and might be blamed for affecting the temperaments of many a once jolly trader! I felt that I had to inform the bookseller of my discovery and retraced my steps to his stall. Holding the book aloft I spoke politely.

'My good man, you may remember that I paid you sixpence for this book but half an hour ago? Well, upon examining it . . .'

Dear reader, I will not sully the page by writing an accurate account of his reply. To say that he was rude and unpleasant is to put it mildly.

After he had poured scorn upon my appearance, my age, my parentage even, he said, 'I sold that book to you for sixpence to be taken exactly as found. Now be off and annoy someone else!'

So you see, dear reader, I had tried to be honest and return that possibly valuable synopsis to the vendor. But he was so very unpleasant that I decided my responsibility in that direction was at an end.

Back home at Camberley I went into my study and spread the yellowing foolscap sheets before me. I could see that the synopsis would make an excellent story and I wondered why Watson had not published it. (For I knew from my experience as a collector that he had not.) Dare I step into the breach and perform the task that Watson had evidently neglected to undertake? My qualifications as far as writing was concerned were confined to a dozen or so books upon zoological subjects: *In Search of the Okapi* and similar titles, yet I felt almost equal to the task. Why though had Watson not written and published *Sherlock Holmes and the Tomb of Terror*, for its content and subject were absorbing. Then I noticed that the manuscript was dated: January 21st 1930. Dr Watson is generally considered by Sherlockians to have passed on in the summer of that same year and possibly failing health had halted his work upon this interesting case of his friend and colleague Sherlock Holmes.

The subject matter, though, was so very different from my usual field, and I hesitated for some time, until inspiration struck. I invited my old friend, Val Andrews, Esq., to collaborate with me, and give the work a final professional polish.

In deciding to take on this task we performed it with reverence and admiration for John H. Watson's wonderful chronicles of his adventures with the world's first and greatest consulting detective. The synopsis was a very full one, which has aided our task. No likeness here to the efforts of those who have attempted to finish Dickens's *Mystery of Edwin Drood* because Watson's manuscript indicates not only the episode's beginning and middle, but also its resolution.

It is to be sincerely hoped that the reader will enjoy reading this adventure as much as we have enjoyed putting the flesh upon its bones.

Colonel George Court, FZS
Camberley, Surrey
July 24th, 1946

CHAPTER ONE

Enter Abdul Faziel

'By Jove, Holmes, you are missing a treat!'

It was the most momentous new year that either of us would live to see, this centennial whereby the nineteenth century was giving way to the twentieth. As a depiction of our beloved Queen could be seen clearly in the sky, thanks to a thousand fireworks, even from our window at 221B Baker Street, I muttered a prayer of thanks that she had been spared to see this brave new century. But Sherlock Holmes would not stir from his fireside armchair to see it, saying, 'Call it what you like, Watson, but the calendar is entirely man-made. There are the seasons and of course occasional variation to give us natural disasters, but mother nature recognises no man-invented dates.'

'But Holmes, there is a likeness of the Queen, lighting up the sky!'

'My dear Watson, we have a splendid portrait of Her Majesty hanging in its place of honour upon our walls. Is the firework likeness as close or detailed?'

I was about to make a rejoinder when I was, perhaps

mercifully, interrupted by Mrs Hudson who knocked and then entered. As she made to speak, Holmes showed the kindly side of his nature which did exist even if the account of our conversation might suggest otherwise. It was he who spoke first. 'My dear Mrs Hudson, may I take this opportunity to wish you a very happy new year, nay new century. Dr Watson and I can face the twentieth century undismayed whilst we have your good and faithful service to rely upon.'

She blushed a little and said, 'I wish you and the Doctor every success in the new year, but if you please, sir, there is a person waiting to see you.'

'You say "person" as if you might not think our caller is a lady or a gentleman. Despite the noise from the street I heard his tread in the hall below. His steps are those of a man, yet they sound as if he wears soft shoes. So by "person" you mean that he is not European?'

'That's right, sir; he is dark, but not like the ones who come performing in the street with banjos; he is lighter in complexion and rather splendid in his dress. As you say, sir, he has soft shoes, like the one you keep your tobacco in, but not so decorative. But Mr Holmes, my only reason for calling him a "person" was because he has no card. Says that his name is Abdul Faziel.'

'Ah, so he is North African.'

I chimed in, 'Not Turkish?'

'I doubt it; the name suggests Egypt or Morocco. But we will soon learn more of him. Pray tell the gentleman that I will see him, Mrs Hudson.'

Abdul Faziel proved to be a young man of Arabic appearance with a stately bearing. He was dressed in a loose robe made of a striped towel-like cloth, his head supported a red tarbush around which a length of cloth had been wound, giving it a turban-like appearance. He wore baggy trousers of blue cloth, partly visible beneath the three-quarter length of his robe. His feet were indeed encased in Eastern-style slippers. He made a low salaam and spoke with the tones of an Arab educated perhaps at Oxford or Cambridge. Holmes showed manners almost as courtly as our visitor's as he bowed him into our best armchair.

Then he called to our good landlady. 'Mrs Hudson, coffee, a large pot, very strong, as black in fact as you can make it.'

Our caller's troubled eyes gleamed with gratitude for a moment. 'Honoured Efendi, you are too kind to this hapless one who comes to you with the troubles of the world upon his shoulders.'

'Aside from rheumatic pains, what troubles do you bring?'

'You can diagnose my rheumatism from my movements?'

'No, though perhaps my friend and colleague, Dr Watson might. But I never met a man from the African continent who did not suffer from our January weather. Can I offer you a cigarette, cigar or tobacco?'

Our visitor took a cigar from the proffered coal scuttle and lit it with a curious device which produced sparks like a flintlock which caused an attached short length of rope to smoulder. Holmes examined it with glee, then commented, 'You are not a disciple of Mohammed, I perceive.'

I asked, 'How can you tell that, Holmes?'

My friend smiled mysteriously. 'Do not from habit assume me to be right, Watson. But I can tell that our friend is permitted by his religion to make contact with tobacco with his lips.'

The dusky one concurred. 'You are right, of course, Mr Holmes. My religion is a very ancient one, going back many thousands of years. We have no taboos concerning tobacco and the manner in which it may be smoked, moreover we are permitted alcoholic beverages. You may not even have heard of Marrafaze.'

'That is your country? Yes, I have heard of it, but only as a vague rumour of a land which exists in the Sahara, but has never been visited by Europeans. So the mysterious Marrafaze is your country, eh?'

'Yes, Mr Holmes, it is difficult to travel to or from, but not impossible as you will gather from my presence. Indeed this is my second visit to Great Britain. I was here some ten years ago to be educated . . .'

'At Cambridge?'

'Why yes, you can tell that I went to Cambridge rather than Oxford?'

'Indeed, moreover I can deduce that you went to Jesus College rather than simply Cambridge.'

Faziel threw up his hands in wonder. 'Upon my word, sir, you can detect that finely my seat of learning from my speech?'

Holmes smiled indulgently. 'Were you British I possibly could not, but as English is not your native tongue you have picked up the vocal tricks of one or two professors of my acquaintance. But sir, please tell me how I can be of service to you?'

Abdul Faziel gratefully sipped a steaming cup of black coffee as he started his oration.

'My father is the Sheikhama of Marrafaze. He is a very old man, he may not even see the year out. As his eldest son

I am heir to the sheikdom. Now sir, you yourself touched upon the isolation of my land and the vagaries of my religion. Imagine Britain before the Christian era; the time of the "old religion" as your isolated yokels still refer to it; the time of straw dollies and witchcraft. We have no one god but a series of them, and they speak to my father through the Grand Wazir who influences him.'

I could see that Sherlock Holmes was growing not so much impatient (for he obviously found what Faziel had to say of great interest), but puzzled as to where the oration was leading. 'Yes Mr Faziel, I can understand how isolated your country must be for such outmoded beliefs and customs to still exist. But how do they affect you, if indeed they affect you at all?'

Abdul Faziel at once took Holmes's hint. 'Of course, sir, forgive my ramblings and I will get straight to the point of my visit; which is an imposition at such an hour and on New Year's Eve. My problem is that my father has been turned against me by the connivance of my brother Mustapha and the Grand Wazir, who would stand to gain much if Mustapha were to sit upon the throne of Marrafaze rather than myself.'

'How so?'

'Well, Mustapha is poorly educated and believes in all that the old religion teaches. Therefore Hassani, the Grand Wazir, would become very powerful should Mustapha succeed; knowing that to influence him would be even easier than it is with my father. Both know that I would try to bring Marrafaze into the modern world, at least as far as influential superstitions are concerned. With this in mind the pair of them have done all they can to discredit me with my father. But the Sheik is loyal to me, as his eldest son, and has not as yet been deeply affected by their evil words. This has turned them to taking stronger methods of eliminating me, to give them a clear field. They set assassins upon me and, whilst my father would still listen to me, he would not believe in my accusations. Life in Marrafaze became dangerous, nay impossible, for me, and I have been forced to flee to the country where I assumed that I would be safe.'

I interjected, 'Have you reason then to believe that is not so?'

'Yes, Hakin Efendi, whilst for the first month of my stay here all was well, I have recently been followed and observed by agents of my brother or the Wazir.'

Holmes nodded. 'It would have taken that long, I imagine, for any sort of word to reach here from Marrafaze?'

'Yes, even then such communication would not have been easy, there being no means of telegraphing between the two places. They would have had to send a letter through a caravan that was making for Bechar, which is near the Moroccan border. The goal for the letter would be the port of Tangier, from which it could eventually reach London. These agents are bad people who perform assassinations. Though for the moment I think they are content to observe my movements.'

I could see that Holmes's interest had been captured and he asked, 'Do you suppose they followed you here?'

Abdul replied, thoughtfully, 'I cannot be sure, but I do not believe they did. Through all the excitement and crowds in the streets I think I evaded them.'

Sherlock Holmes pondered before he spoke further. At last he pronounced, 'Mr Faziel, from what you have told me no actual crime has been committed, save possibly that of defamation of character. Until such time as your shadowers actually attempt to do you some kind of physical harm, it is difficult to see where I could enter this drama.'

'But esteemed sir, I have funds of my own in London with which I could pay you to effect my protection.'

'Come, sir, you could enlist the help of the police, who would charge you nothing to tell you exactly what I have told you myself. Until some sort of actual threat is issued there is nothing to be done. I will however give you my advice, for which I will charge you no fee. Where are you staying?'

'At a small hotel in the vicinity of the British Museum.'

'Then may I suggest that you do not return there, but take up residence elsewhere, perhaps near Baker Street, so that you can quickly contact me if an actual threat should occur, always assuming that they find you at all.'

'They found me quickly enough where I am now.'

'Exactly, because they knew perhaps where you had stayed when in London before. Break new ground and you may be rid of them. May I suggest that you stay at the Exeter, a guest house in this very street where I am known. Register there as Septimus Jones. The proprietor will raise no eye-brow if you mention my name. Watson will lend you a carpet bag and a few necessities; tomorrow you can of course purchase whatever you need.'

Our visitor was much calmed by Holmes's words and agreed to take his advice. I was enlisted to accompany him to the Exeter and have a quiet word with the landlord who knew me almost as well as he knew Holmes.

'A happy new century to you, my dear Watson!'

These were the words which greeted my late arrival at the breakfast table on the first day of 1900. Sherlock Holmes had for once demolished a hearty breakfast as he turned upon me a gimlet glance of accusation. I had already broken my resolve for the new year and he knew it, despite the fact that I had mentioned no such thing as punctuality. I grunted, returned the greeting and looked for letters upon my plate. There were none, but I noticed that Holmes had two or three. These proved unremarkable; a tailor's bill which I knew would be promptly paid, an advice note from a bookseller and an as yet unopened brown paper envelope.

'What do you make of this, Watson, you know my methods . . .'

I took the brown envelope and studied it carefully. 'Delivered by hand, Holmes, for it bears no stamp or post mark. Looks like a child has addressed it; perhaps a delayed Christmas card from a young admirer? Indeed this seems borne out by the fact that the envelope has been home-made from a piece of brown paper. Only a child would manufacture an envelope, surely?'

'Anything else?'

'Not really, except that there are some stains upon the brown paper, probably from the jammy fingers of the sender.'

'Well done, Watson, a perfect example of misinterpretation.'

'I haven't got it quite right, eh?'

'Quite right? Why, my dear fellow, your deductions are wrong from beginning to end. Let us begin with the home-made envelope; it is indeed made up from a piece of brown paper, but it has been well and neatly done so that one would have to look twice to realise that it had not been purchased. Certainly not the work of a child and, by the way, the stains are those left my some gum, accidentally deposited there in the adhesion of the flaps.' He raised the envelope to his great beak of a nose. 'Stevens' Mucilage I suspect; and the writing is that of an adult, unused to writing fluently in the English language.'

I said nothing as he slit the envelope with a butter knife and extracted a piece of white card which he removed with some difficulty, for it was clear that the envelope had been made around the card, a snug fit. He perused it for a short while and then passed it to me. I studied it carefully.

'HOLMES SIR,
DO NOT CONCERN YOURSELF WITH THE AFFAIRS OF ABDUL FAZIEL.
GREAT HARM CAN COME TO YOU IF YOU HEED NOT THIS WARNING!
DISCIPLES OF THE WAZIR'

Holmes spoke first. 'Well, Watson, what do you make of that?'

'That Abdul was after all shadowed here, and that whoever followed him knew you by reputation, for your door bears no name plate.'

'Exactly, and he must likewise have followed you both to the Exeter and knows that Faziel is domiciled there. Come, Watson, we must take ourselves to the Exeter and make sure that all is well with our new client.'

'You have decided to take on his case then?'

'I have no alternative, Watson; I really cannot have people threatening me, or telling me what or what not to do!'

My friend was already formally attired, but I needed to forsake my robe in favour of my coat and greatcoat; for although the Exeter was only a short walk away, the January chill was upon us. Within ten minutes we were sitting inside Abdul's bed chamber and he and Holmes were in earnest conversation.

'My dear Holmes, Efendi, you have changed your mind and will help me?'

'Let us say, Faziel, that I will give the matter thought and concern.'

Holmes walked to the window, looked without and about him before he spoke again. Then he asked, 'Do you think you could write the names of any people in your own country who might be involved in plotting against you?'

He passed his small pad and pencil to Abdul for him to write upon, and as this was being done Holmes moved around the room, seemingly in pensive mood, but I knew from my experience of him that he took in every detail. Then, after a few minutes, Abdul returned the pad and pencil to Holmes who studied what he had written thereon. He nodded, and placed the pad upon the bedside table, casually dropping the threatening missive, which he had extracted from his pocket, beside it.

'Faziel, I perceive you were about at an early hour.'

'How can you tell that, honoured sir?'

'Why from the fact that you are wearing a brand-new shirt and collar. You had no luggage with you last night, and I'll wager I know Watson's linen well enough to know that you are not wearing a shirt of his!'

'So right, I was lucky to catch a very early bird of a trader who sold it to me, along with the collar. You see, Dr Watson's shirt proved a little large for me. I have always worn European-style linen, even beneath my native garb. A shirt needs to be changed daily if one is to feel comfortable.'

Holmes nodded, and I wondered why he concerned himself with Abdul's linen. But I was soon to learn why.

'Do you have the packing in which you took the shirt from the trader?'

'Why, yes, I believe it is in the waste bucket . . .'

'Do not trouble yourself, I will find it.'

Holmes delved in the waste bucket and fished out brown wrapping paper, and piece of white card which the trader had used to pack and stiffen the shirt. My friend examined these, to me, petty objects carefully.

'You see, Watson, a small piece of white card has been cut from this piece which was intended to stiffen the shirt and make it more attractive for sale. You will observe also that a rather larger piece has been cut from the brown wrapping.'

Abdul started, saying, 'Why, I suppose both the paper and card were trimmed down by the trader better to fit the shirt?'

I said, 'Perhaps so, but really Holmes, I fail to see what difference it makes.'

Sherlock Holmes looked stern as he spoke. 'Mr Faziel, the piece of white card upon which the threatening message was written exactly fits the missing portion of the shirt stiffener.'

'Does it? Goodness . . .'

Faziel was short of words but full of embarrassment.

Holmes continued. 'The brown wrapping paper is also missing a piece at one end; observe where it has been cut, and I'll wager it was used to manufacture an envelope. You should have invested in card and envelope at the same shop where you obtained the Stevens' Mucilage, my dear Faziel! By the way, although your writing is quite different from the uneducated scrawl of the message and envelope there are still a few characteristics which you have failed to disguise. For example, the slim double vee which forms the W for the "Wazir" on both your list and the message.'

There was a silence that you could have cut with a knife. Faziel stood, head bowed, unable to meet the accusing gimlet eyes of Sherlock Holmes. As for myself, I was astounded, for I could see that Holmes must be right in what he had revealed. Yet he made no accusation, he just asked, 'Why, Faziel?'

'Fear!'

The son of the Sheik spoke up and raised his eyes to meet those of the detective boldly.

'It was wrong of you to try to force my hand by seeming to involve me with your enemies but I admire your enterprise. The fear you mention must be very real to have moved your deception, or rather your attempt at such. If I have your word that you will never try to deceive me again I will help you with your problems. You see, these idiotic attempts to beguile me rather make me believe that you have no experience of deception.'

We left Faziel at the Exeter and made our way back to 221B. As we walked, I asked, 'Holmes, why did Faziel not buy a card and envelope instead of the mucilage?'

My friend chuckled. 'You should have asked him that, Watson, but old habits die hard and I'll wager there are very few stationers' shops in Marrafaze!'

Back at our rooms Holmes surrounded himself with maps and albums in order to acquaint himself with all possible details concerning Marrafaze. At length he said, 'I am intrigued, Watson, I am indeed intrigued. Friend Faziel declared that his country was all but legendary. Well, according to all that I can find upon the subject, Marrafaze is believed by quite eminent explorers to be a figment of an explorer's imagination. Yet if Faziel is to be believed, and I think he is, he has made the journey between there and Britain more than once. There must be an authority upon world affairs and geography that I can consult upon the subject.'

He selected a straight briar from among his pipes and filled it with a coarse shag, and soon the room was like a railway waiting room. Then after he had worked hard upon the pipe for twenty minutes without further consulting book or atlas he leapt to his feet and shouted, 'Mycroft!'

I wondered at his shouting of his brother's name for a second or two, but then I began to realise why he had done so. Mycroft Holmes was a man with connections with the British government. There had been times when for short periods he had not only represented, but actually was Her Majesty's government. Holmes expanded, 'Mycroft knows every dukedom, sheikdom and tin-pot government on earth and has had dealings with places that few have even heard of. If anyone can give me unbiased information regarding Marrafaze, it is he.'

CHAPTER TWO

The Diplomats

The Major Domo outside the Diogenes Club looked at us askance as we made to enter those august premises. He gave us a somewhat hesitant salute which seemed to mean 'I don't know you, but you look respectable enough, and could be more important than you look.' Inside we mounted the vast marble staircase and made our way up to the Stranger's Room where we knew that we would almost certainly find Mycroft lounging elegantly in his favourite chair. This proved to be so and although Mycroft was glad to see us he made no sign of attempting to rise from his chair. He moved his arms in a vast gesture of hospitality which quickly produced a waiter. Like some elegant sea lion Mycroft Holmes caused the waiter to fetch refreshments for us all.

Then once we were comfortably seated he spoke with that tone of authority and diplomacy for which he was justly famous. 'My dear Sherlock, I hear of you everywhere. Watson, I believe it is at least partly due to your efforts that I do hear of Sherlock everywhere. It is wonderful to see you both, but I imagine you have not called upon me to pass the time of the day? If there is anything that I can do for you, please do not hesitate to mention it; in fact mention it by all means.'

As we sat comfortably and smoked our cigars Holmes gave Mycroft some ideas of the events of the past few hours. Mycroft took it all in with a surprising display of interest. He glanced out through the large window saying, 'You know of course that you have been followed here?'

Sherlock Holmes surprised me by his reply. 'You mean by the Arab in the European dress, with the billycock at odds with his greatcoat?'

'My interest is more with the German who is holding subdued conversation with him.'

Sherlock glanced through the window. 'Oh, you mean the gentleman who is in the secret service of the German government?'

I glanced at the pair who stood upon the opposite pavement. I asked, 'How do you know that he is a secret service man?'

Sherlock replied, 'He is sedately dressed yet appears ill at ease in his clothing. Notice how he repeatedly hunches his shoulders to ease the fit of a greatcoat that was not made for him. He is typical of his kind, he carries a revolver.'

I asked, 'How do you know that he is not just some common criminal?'

It was Mycroft who replied. 'If he were, the bulge caused by the revolver would be just inside the breast of his coat, giving a typically one-sided appearance.'

Sherlock agreed. 'You will notice, Watson, the slight

bulge at his hip. An extremely impractical place to carry such a weapon, a professional criminal would never do it.'

Mycroft rather fussily put his brother right on a technical point. 'He is, by the way, Prussian; you will notice the way his cravat has been knotted in the style of a Prussian cavalryman in civilian dress.'

'Non-commissioned, do you not think?'

'Undoubtedly. An officer would have tied a smaller, tighter knot.'

The two astute brothers continued in this fashion for some time. Some of the finer points were lost on me as far as their importance was concerned, but the general theme of a collusion between subversives of Arabian and Germanic origins I could appreciate. To my relief Sherlock Holmes confessed to his brother that there was an aspect of it all that he could not understand.

'I rather fail to see, my dear Mycroft, one thing and that is where this connection of agents from two continents comes into the picture.'

Mycroft was sympathetic rather than triumphant in manner as he explained, 'There is little chance that you could have known. The two governments, those of Her Majesty and of the Kaiser, are at present equally interested in the Sheikdom, or rumoured Sheikdom, of Marrafaze. Just why I am not at liberty to divulge, even to my own brother.'

'So it really does, as I have been convinced by friend Abdul, exist?'

'You were not wrong to believe his story; for he did indeed obtain his education at Cambridge and is not unknown to us. Your account of the domestic differences in the family may or may not have some bearing on what we are trying to bring about. But of course your report when you return from Marrafaze will be invaluable.'

I started, for I did not believe that Sherlock Holmes had agreed to any such perilous journey. My friend, although he did not turn a hair at Mycroft's words, laid his cards very firmly upon the table. 'My dear Mycroft, you assume too much! I have not as yet agreed to look into Faziel's problem. I have merely been trying to protect him from immediate danger; but even that attention is no longer required as I feel sure that your people are now guarding him?'

Mycroft Holmes was unperturbed by his brother's words. He leaned back in his chair, crossing one huge leg over the other and spoke very quietly.

'Sherlock, what if I were to tell you that to send someone to Marrafaze and make diplomatic contact with the Sheik is absolutely vital to your country? The enemies of the Sheik, his eldest son and ourselves already doubtless know of your involvement. But they know nothing of me, or my connection with the government. This means that Watson and yourself could go there, masquerading as diplomat and aide without their immediate knowledge of it. When you go there they will believe that your only aim is to plead Abdul's case with his father the Sheik. But once there you could present papers that I will prepare for you and it would be quite a time before anyone knew about it outside of Marrafaze. Yet within that Sheikdom a treaty would have been signed, a treaty with which I will furnish you, which you will have brought back to me before anyone in Europe is any the wiser.'

We were, of course, rather taken aback by this beautifully

and, I thought, rather craftily delivered speech of Mycroft's.

There was a short silence before Holmes eventually replied, 'You are assuming then that our trek to Marrafaze is a *fait accompli*, Mycroft; a somewhat cavalier attitude upon your part, I consider. I have a number of matters which I presently wish to pursue here in London and I feel sure that Watson cannot for ever be finding others to undertake his medical duties. You bring Her Majesty into the affair as a form of blackmail?'

Mycroft smiled as he answered, '*Touché*, brother mine, but let me tell you that only yesterday I was consulting with the Prime Minister upon the subject of Marrafaze . . .' Mycroft lowered his voice to a whisper as he continued . . . 'Sherlock, he admitted to me that despite every diplomatic effort that will continue, a great European war, something on the scale that the world has never seen, is inevitable. Now there is in Marrafaze, reputedly, a certain mineral, found nowhere else as far as we know, which would make such a conflict extremely one-sided. If the Germans get hold of it and sign a treaty before us, we may be doomed or at best enslaved. But if we can make such a treaty the conflict could not just be won, but possibly avoided entirely.'

Holmes was impassive. 'Why, Mycroft, do you not go yourself?'

Mycroft laughed openly. 'My dear Sherlock, just look at me! Do you see a man who is capable of crossing the Sahara, on a camel, or, should he survive, arriving in Marrafaze in a fit state to carry out diplomatic duties in the face of conspiracy among the ruler's aides? But you and Watson are capable of doing this job, and have the perfect blind. If you refuse I will quite understand: indeed I will not hold it against you, though perhaps I might be forgiven if I were never able to hold you in such great esteem again.'

There was a long and dangerous silence, broken eventually by Sherlock's words. 'You leave me, by your words, no alternative but to go to Marrafaze, Mycroft. But feelings between us can never be quite the same again.'

'How so? I will be full of admiration for you always!'

'You assume, do you, that such feelings will be reciprocated?'

The elder Holmes nodded wisely. 'It is a sacrifice that I must make for my country. To lose the respect of my younger brother is a heavy price indeed for me to pay. But perhaps I will be able to regain it?'

Sherlock nodded grimly. 'Time will tell, which reminds me that time is something which is no longer on our side, Watson. We will leave and prepare to journey to Marrafaze, should that be possible for us. I leave you to make most of the arrangements, Mycroft.'

To see him nod curtly to his own brother as we departed was something that I would never have expected Sherlock Holmes to do.

As we climbed into a hansom, Holmes spoke quietly. 'Watson, I have landed you perhaps in something you would rather avoid. I have committed myself, but no one can make you take part in this escapade; my friend, believe me when I say that I would not dream of exerting such pressure on you as I have suffered myself. If you are either unable or unwilling to accompany me, not only will I not hold it against you but would never let the fact spoil our long friendship. You are my only friend and I believe will be ever so.'

I had already considered my position so I was able to say, 'You know I will go with you, Holmes. I am no diplomat but I have some experience of desert travel which might prove useful.'

'Not just useful, Watson, but invaluable, I'll wager!'

The two days that followed were filled with activity for us both. I had to arrange discreetly for a locum to attend my cases, whilst Holmes conferred with Mrs Hudson concerning his impending protracted absence. He also needed to inform Faziel of our plan to visit his country, allowing him to believe that it was entirely connected with his domestic problems. Inspector Lestrade of Scotland Yard was consulted and agreed to ensure Abdul's safety at the Exeter. But most important of all was our visit to the Foreign Office where we were to receive the treaty as well as confer with the minister. We had made no secret of our activities save in this one instance. Holmes conspired with Lestrade to have two police officers who corresponded with our general heights and appearance secreted in a hansom. They crouched low as we clambered in and from a distance it would have been difficult for their presence to be detected. In similar morning clothes and headgear they climbed out as the hansom stopped at the Diogenes Club, entering that building swiftly. Our shadowers were deceived and stood upon the pavement as before. The police driver of the bogus cab whipped up the horse so that once out of their sight we could straighten up.

I sighed with relief. 'That went off well, Holmes. I don't fancy we are still being trailed.'

Holmes agreed that it was unlikely and we were shortly

entering the Foreign Office where the minister awaited us. I will not test the reader's patience by reporting the conversation which took place between the three of us for the minister repeated, almost word for word that which Mycroft had already said to us, save for those remarks concerning family loyalty. But we got an extra large slice of loyalty to Her Majesty. The treaty was given to us in a special pouch and Holmes also received a letter, signed by the minister, which was to give us free passage throughout our journey. Then the police hansom took us to that store in the Strand, renowned for its stock of tropical rainment for explorers and soldiers.

Holmes left the choice of such items to me, relying on my experiences in India and Afghanistan. Of course the continent was different but some of the conditions I knew would be similar. The desert I knew would be blisteringly hot by day and cruelly cold by night. With this in mind I picked out tropical tunics and breeches and thick woollen robes for us both. Boots and puttees for protection from sand and snakes, absorbent woollen socks and plenty of suitable undergarments. I picked out a suitable belt holster for my service revolver and stocked up with ammunition. A small strong army-style tent and water carafes completed our purchases, save for one large metal trunk which would carry all save the tent. Then, remembering some of my experiences as a soldier of the Queen, I procured from the same store a number of canvas satchels in case no cart was available to carry the trunk. They were the sort of things in which one could pack everything in order to hang them from asses' saddles or camel howdahs. Knives, forks, plates and spoons, also mugs, all of enamelled metal completed our equipment.

Holmes's face was a study as I selected these items, but he made no objective to anything that I chose, save in the single instance of a sun helmet. I had selected two pith helmets with rear-hanging sun protection. But Holmes handed his helmet back to the salesman, saying, 'I don't mind having to use all this other ridiculous paraphernalia, but I refuse to wear a pukka sahib headgear! Perhaps I can obtain here a wide brimmed hat of felt, as worn by pioneers in the west of the Americas?'

I humoured my friend in choosing for him a suitable hat which would have brought joy to the heart of any cowboy or bushranger! I have to admit that he cut quite a dashing figure in it. There was something about this wide brimmed hat that suited his aquiline features.

In the event my choices were to prove extremely practical and Holmes would live to thank me for my sagacity concerning at least some of my choices.

We got our purchases back to 221B Baker Street where Billy assisted the cab driver to take the box trunk up the stairs. Mrs Hudson surprised Holmes whilst he was trying on his wide brimmed hat and was quite captivated by the sight he presented.

She threw her apron up in front of her face and peeped over its hem in delight. 'Upon my word, Mr Holmes, you are not going to join Colonel Cody's Wild West Show, are you?'

But I felt that the addition of a straight briar between his teeth gave him more the appearance of a Voortrekker! As for myself, I was at home in the pith helmet; indeed there was a photograph of myself in such headgear upon our mantelpiece. It was somewhat faded, despite being behind glass in a frame, but a glance at it always brought back the moment of its taking, or I should say minutes of its taking, for despite the strong sunlight the exposure was a long one in those early days of photography. Today the camera operator can capture an image in perhaps two or three seconds, so his subject does not have that agonised expression assumed by those who had to keep perfectly still for perhaps half a minute.

But there were serious matters to be discussed. Holmes began to lay out our plan of action that very evening, working out our itinery in some detail. His large-scale maps of Europe and North Africa were spread large as he planned our route.

'We shall take the boat train to Paris, travelling from there into Spain, eventually reaching Gibraltar, from where we will cross the straits to Tangier.'

He made it sound so easy, but as a seasoned traveller I knew it would not be so. I knew that the journey across the vast seas of sand to the legendary Marrafaze would also be far from easy. In fact, other than Abdul Faziel, we would be hard put to find another who had actually made the journey. Did Holmes really intend to leave Abdul in London rather than use his invaluable services as a guide? I could not believe that he did, yet saw the wisdom of his words when he said, 'His advice will be invaluable, but I cannot take him with us, for I rely upon his presence here to delay those who will undoubtedly eventually follow in our wake. He will be our decoy, Watson. He and the two detectives who helped us before will leave together in a hurry and lead our tormentors a merry chase, leaving us a goodly start, an excellent advantage. With no means of communication between Marrafaze and the outside world we may even have performed our tasks, which are several, before they even reach that place or cause their minions to do so. Lestrade's actors are good at their work, they could keep up the masquerade for longer than one might think. We could have reached Tangier before our ruse is discovered.'

'You think then, Holmes, that the use once already of this method will not make it obvious?'

'Obvious? Not at all, for I'll wager that they are still wondering how we managed to give them the slip before. Although the German is an experienced agent, it was well done and I believe he was as deceived as his Arab companion.'

As part of Holmes's plan we took to visiting Abdul at the Exeter at regular intervals, always clad in our most personally distinctive rainment: Holmes in his deerstalker and Inverness cape in which friend Paget had immortalised him, whilst I wore a military-style greatcoat and suitably matching hat. Our acting might well have worried Sir Henry Irving, for we were well muffled against the cold, yet allowed our features to be seen as if by accident, hastily turning our collars up. Although we did not see those who watched us, we instinctively knew that they were there, observing us.

We, of course, told Abdul that which delighted him: that Holmes would indeed be taking up his case and therefore making the dangerous and difficult journey to Marrafaze. But we told him nothing of the other implications, the international importance of our errand or that Holmes was being all but blackmailed into going by his own brother. Although he might for all we knew have been able to give us some information regarding the all-important mineral, no mention was made of it. I felt rather ashamed when our dark-skinned friend lavished his thanks upon us. 'Mr Holmes, Efendi, I cannot thank you enough for putting aside your works of great importance to help me with my unworthy problem. Dr Watson, you too are such a good man, and I am unworthy of such magnificent kindness.'

Although in my heart I cringed, I could only say, 'Not at all, think nothing of it.'

Abdul was delighted with the ruse that we had planned. He was fortunately a highly intelligent man and could grasp the benefit of that which we had planned; or that of it which we cared to impart to him. We said nothing about the German agent, and fortunately he did not appear to have seen anything strange in another European presence, thinking, perhaps, that the German had been enlisted locally by his tormentors.

Our baggage we had taken to Victoria by cab whilst we were performing one of our histrionic escapades at the Exeter. Mrs Hudson and Billy supervised this as quietly as they could. Thus when the time had finally arrived for us to leave we were able to make an inconspicuous departure, quietly dressed, and hail a hansom to take us to Victoria several streets from our rooms.

Mycroft had provided us with many items: travel documents for 'Socrates Holbrook' and 'Professor Julian Westlake'. I noticed that our initials were unchanged and appreciated the wisdom of this, for it made the desperate last-minute shielding of cufflinks and watch initials unnecessary.

During our long conversations with Abdul we had learned all that we could regarding his father, the Sheik, the Grand Wazir and all the intrigue that existed in Marrafaze. But upon the matter of that mineral which might make a difference to the future of mankind it was wise for us to say little or nothing. I knew in my heart that Holmes believed that Mycroft had overestimated the importance of this 'something', whatever it might be. Fate had played a strange game, dealt a hand to us which had made decision where there had been doubt; complicated the issue in general yet greatly simplified our path to Marrafaze itself.

When the starting pistol of my imagination fired, Holmes turned to me as we sat in the cab and spoke those words, so well remembered from past adventure curtain raisers yet never before spoken by him in a single sentence . . .

'Come, my dear Watson, the game is afoot, but we are both stoutly shod and you have your service revolver!'

The train journeys to and through France were uneventful save in that Holmes kept an eagle eye cocked for any pursuit. When we reached Paris he was fairly sure that we had not been followed, but to make sure he arranged for us to be put off the Toulouse-bound train at what we in Great Britain would call a 'Halt'. The dismay I felt at the sight of that train, disappearing at an alarming rate in the direction of a good dinner and a comfortable night's sleep was allayed a little by the fact that we were quite alone and clearly unmarked by shadowy trackers.

We were able to hire a donkey cart which took us to Tarbes, from where Holmes had worked out that we could get a train, on the morrow, for Madrid. That night we stayed at a farmhouse and were given a dish of paella each, of such a quality that seemed to merge the culinary aspects of France and Spain. We washed it down with wine that was definitely French in character and I slept as well as the fieldmice in the thatch would allow.

The train journey to Madrid was a long one and the train was rather primitive and overcrowded, but we were able to purchase refreshments from a number of itinerant traders whenever the train stopped. We no longer felt that we needed to be alert in case we were shadowed. As for Madrid itself, I was surprised to find that despite our late arrival there we were able to wander round shops and take coffee at Parisian-style pavement café tables. As we sat there, well wrapped against the chill of the evening, a peasant woman, much of the upper part of her frame enveloped in a black shawl, attempted to read our palms. She was shrewd enough and I soon realised that she was telling us that which we wanted to hear. She told me for example that I was a military man and that I had enjoyed a promising career cut short by being wounded in battle. She was puzzled by Holmes, eventually categorising him as a cleric; probably through an observation of his austere appearance, free of any form of decorative adornment.

But my friend turned the tables neatly by taking her hand and examining her palm with interest. 'What do you see in this palm, Watson?'

I decided to play up, pretended to study her palm closely before stating the obvious. 'She is of Romany extraction, but several generations of her family have dwelt in Spain. She is happily married, with several children. She comes from a devoutly religious Catholic family. Most of her time is spent in reading palms.'

Holmes chuckled and said, 'Excellent, Watson, you are right as to her gypsy origin and I have no doubt that she has several children.'

I was puzzled when he stopped speaking. 'Does your

abrupt cessation of comment mean that I am wrong in saying that she is happily married, from a highly devout family and that her fortune telling occupies a great deal of her time?'

Before giving you Holmes's reply I should tell the reader that our conversation between ourselves was in English, but we spoke to her in Spanish. Thus we were free to discuss the poor woman.

Holmes continued, 'That she is herself a devout Catholic is obvious from certain articles of jewellery that she wears; for example, the crucifix at her neck. Possibly her parents shared this devotion but I rather think that her husband does not and that in consequence the marriage is not a happy one.'

'How can you tell this simply from the fact that she wears a crucifix about her neck?'

'Not perhaps from that fact alone, Watson, but if you use your eyes you will see that the chain on the crucifix has been broken and carefully repaired with thin wire. Notice also the corresponding wound, now healed but fairly recent, at her neck. The crucifix has been savagely seized and torn from her neck, wounding her and breaking the chain. I would wager that the quarrel was concerned with religion, so she may be married to one of different faith or none at all. She has spirit and has mended the chain as best she could.'

I could see the logic of his words but he had left gaps in explaining away my deductions. 'The use of her time other than to read palms?'

'Did you not notice the ends of her fingers? Countless tiny cuts, some recent, many more healed. She is regularly employed in the manufacture of certain objects. My knowledge of the Romany people suggests to me that she makes clothes pegs.'

I was still a little sceptical and said as much. 'Come, Holmes, I know your methods, yet I have seen you use them to more convincing effect.'

Holmes handed the woman a generous amount in pesetas and that could well have been the end of the matter had not a rough-looking gypsy man in a fur jacket and leather breeches come onto the scene. He grabbed the woman roughly by the wrist and started to shout at her in what I took to be Romany. He had seen her stuff the money that Holmes had given her into a pochette at her waist. He appeared to be demanding that she hand it to him but this she appeared unwilling to do. Then he made a great mistake by striking her around the mouth with the back of his hand. She backed away from him and appeared undismayed despite a trickle of blood from her lip. His mistake? Well, despite his monastic way of life, my friend has the very greatest respect for women and I have never known him to hold back when a woman was being abused, this occasion being no exception. He rose from his seat and made toward the cowardly ruffian who turned to meet him, somewhat surprised. In Spanish he demanded that Holmes mind his business. But this, of course, Holmes was unwilling to do. My friend squared up to the fellow with fists held high. The gypsy gaped at him in amazement, having possibly expected some reaction, but he had perhaps never experienced the calm irateness of an English gentleman. His response was to take a large knife from his belt and to make threatening movements with it.

But as the Spaniard extended the knife with his right hand, the left fist of one of the finest amateur boxers of his weight struck him in the chest with such force that the knife was dropped. I dashed forward, picking it up and removing it from the scene of action. Holmes nodded to me his gratitude for this move and his own confidence in the result of the encounter. Once disarmed the gypsy had no chance against a rain of lightning blows. It was but a matter of time before he went down and when he did Holmes stood smartly aside, waiting to see if he would arise to continue the fight. This did not happen, so Holmes resumed his seat and casually finished his coffee. The woman appeared to be safely out of sight, but of course I feared for her future welfare.

Madrid by night was quite a revelation with its bright lights and what seemed like a thousand flamenco cafés. The narrow streets with their mellowed buildings reminded me of Spain's Moorish past, while other than in its architecture it was reminiscent of certain parts of the city of London, those few streets that were spared the great fire of 1666. There was so much around to interest me that I had quite forgotten to ask Holmes regarding our next journey. My commonsense had told me that we were working our way toward the part of Spain that was only a few sea miles from North Africa and that he had taken this route to avoid our scent being picked up by those who would even now be in pursuit of us. In fact I asked about those who would show us unwelcome attention.

'We have had a good start, Watson, but our pursuers might possibly have reached Paris by now. I think the German at least will ultimately guess our destination.'

'Do you think it was safe to leave Abdul being observed by them?'

'I am not unduly concerned for his safety with Lestrade watching over him. He is a pedestrian policeman, but very painstaking when presented with a task. We can proceed to Gibraltar on the morrow without fear for Abdul or ourselves. That was the question that you were about to ask me, was it not Watson, our immediate destination?'

I knew enough of geography to know, without consulting an atlas, that Tangier must be Holmes's goal. But I knew of course that Tangier would bring us only within perhaps five hundred miles of our ultimate destination, Marrafaze. We had been convinced by Faziel and Mycroft Holmes that it existed: but few would have believed us.

CHAPTER THREE

Toward the Great Sahara

'So, you are negotiating with the Froggies, what?'
The question came from a Major Kenyon who had lavished much of his time upon us in a tour of the British Garrison at Gibraltar. Like other officials he had been given to believe that we were upon a diplomatic mission to Marrakesh.

I replied, 'We hope they will allow us to start an excavation which could turn up artefacts, proving that there were British soldiers in Morocco as long ago as the crusades.'

I had thought my little deception to be a skilled one but Holmes did not, judging by the way he glowered at me. However, he could only concur once my words had been spoken and Kenyon at least was enthusiastic.

'By Jove! If you could prove that we might have a claim to stake there, what?'

Holmes merely smiled enigmatically and I took his hint and did the same, pretending to take a great interest in the famous rock, which we were forced to climb in order to see the renowned apes. Although so called I could see that they were in fact monkeys of the macaque group, and there were about a score of them, including females with young. Holmes surveyed the monkeys and pointed to a large male animal.

'When did you bring the darker one over from North Africa?'

The major coloured slightly. 'They are native to the rock, sir, the only wild monkeys in Europe.'

Holmes smiled benevolently. 'Oh come, Major, they are an introduced species from North Africa, hopelessly inbred and only thrive at all through occasional additions to their number from across the straits. Over a few hundred years they have developed characteristics of their own with which the dark one differs slightly. But cheer up, Major, the casual observer would never notice the difference.'

I was frankly puzzled by the conversation that accompanied our feeding corn stalks to the monkeys.

I enquired, 'Is it important that they thrive?'

But it was Holmes who answered for the embarrassed soldier. 'It has long been said that when the apes have left Gibraltar the British will have to follow them. They were probably introduced by the Moors and these are the surviving descendants of a group brought here in the Middle Ages. I have heard of no evidence to show that they existed here in prehistoric times. But Professor, you could perhaps tell us more about that?'

His eyes gleamed with mischief as he spoke. I managed some sort of reply, 'Oh quite so, no evidence that I know of . . .'

The major was more at ease now. 'Well, gentlemen, whilst there can be nothing substantial in that old adage there is little point in tempting fate, what?'

That evening we dined with the colonel of the garrison and it was soon obvious that my lapse had filtered through to him. As we tackled an excellent roast goose he said, lowering his voice, 'A little bird has told me that you might be able to put one over on old Pierre, what?'

He touched his bulbous red nose in a rather unattractive gesture, blowing gently through his large white moustache, awaiting our reply.

Holmes waded in, perhaps in order to frustrate a further *faux pas* on my part. He could of course have been serene had he known that I had no intention of saying anything. 'My colleague intimated as much to your Major Kenyon, Colonel, in order to reserve for your own ears the real purpose of our expedition. Really we are involved in a plot on the part of a certain foreign power to capture the apes from the rock. I need hardly tell you what tragedy could follow their abduction?'

The colonel was all but apoplectic. 'My dear Mr Holbrook, Professor Westlake, I had not realised the vital importance of your mission. Count upon my co-operation in every way possible. I could send you to Algiers in my own private yacht.'

Holmes brightened and said, 'If we could be away upon it at the next tide you would indeed be doing your country a great service, Colonel. I shall in fact mention you in my report.'

After that, our departure from Gibraltar and arrival in Algiers went like proverbial clockwork.

The Algiers waterfront proved to be as unsettling as any other busy port but our papers spared us the tribulations that beset the tourist. Despite the presence of so many Arabs, the French influence was marked. We were ushered into a brougham of a kind seldom seen in London for many a year and an Arabian major domo brandished a cane to keep away a horde of traders, money changers and water sellers. The aged white horse with its sun-bonnet hauled the equally elderly equipage the mile or so to the delights of the 'Hotel Splendide'.

Again, although we noted a distinct French influence, the hotel was largely manned by Moroccans. The manager, however, who came scuttling out to greet us once our diplomatic status had been hinted at, was patently French. Moreover Claude Duvalier spoke English with a skill which made me ashamed of my schoolboy French. We had considered the possibility of *The Strand* being available in North Africa, but felt that it would probably not be popular enough to make any form of physical disguise necessary. Imagine then our chagrin when Duvalier pointed to a rack of English periodicals which included *The Strand*. He said, 'Gentlemen, your faces both seem familiar to Duvalier. Does my name ring any sort of bell in your esteemed brain boxes? You see I know the English sayings, having worked for several years at the Charing Cross Hotel in London.'

I prayed that he had not become a reader of *The Strand* and that if he had he would not have followed the exploits and adventures of my friend as chronicled by myself. More than that I hoped he had not recognised us from a study of Paget's brilliant illustrations.

Holmes must have had the same thought because he said to the manager, 'Perhaps you served us in some capacity at the Charing Cross Hotel? Forgive me if I do not at once bring your own face to mind but my sight is extremely poor. As for Professor Westlake, he is in the manner of his kind, extremely absent minded.'

As we followed the Arabian porters who carried our box and other luggage up a wide marble staircase I hoped that Holmes's ruse was a success. I glanced back to see Duvalier shrugging in an amiable manner. Perhaps he would put the whole matter out of his mind within a short while.

As for the accommodation itself, I cannot speak too highly of it. Our room was a very large one by European standards with two huge beds at far sides of the apartment, an ottoman and various moorish tables and seating cushions covered with goatskin. The floor was tiled and the walls were of white plaster. There were huge apertures where one would normally expect glazed windows, fitted with ornamental bars to prevent intruders. Shutters which could be fastened on the inside of these apertures were there, I conjectured, for use during periodic sandstorms or other extremes of weather, or perhaps in a case of rioting in the streets. The room was some fourteen feet high and divided by ornamental archways spanned by beams of some kind of local wood. Once the porters had departed I relaxed and glanced around the room with pleasure. But I suddenly started at a movement upon one of the beams. It was a reptile, quite the biggest lizard that I had encountered.

I pointed at the thing and said, 'Holmes, look up there. Do you see what I do or is it the result of the Algerian wine?'

He chuckled. 'No, Watson, your sobriety is not in doubt. What you see is a small example of an iguana-type giant lizard found only in this part of North Africa. They are tolerated because they have a short way with the rodents which also abound in these parts; everything from the gerboa-type desert rat to the European house mouse which has unfortunately spread to all parts of the globe. The lizard is harmless, I assure you.'

I glanced up at the creature, noting its claws and teeth, and muttered, 'I think I would prefer the desert rats!'

We had been resting in our apartment for some thirty to forty minutes when a rather dramatic interruption occurred. We had heard what sounded rather like a group of booted officials marching around in the corridor.

I had remarked, 'They do have revolutions in this part of the world, Holmes!'

My friend had replied, 'Too well drilled for revolutionaries I feel, Watson. A party of officials is at work here and from what I can hear they seem to be searching each room. It is to be hoped that Mycroft's letter of diplomatic immunity will save us indignity.'

This proved to be so. The French police officer in charge of a group of half a dozen gendarmes saluted and was polite enough, but insisted that he would need to search us, and the room, also our luggage and effects. He presented his own credentials and received the papers which Holmes presented with some surprise. He said, 'Ah, diplomatic immunity, but surely you have nothing to hide, Mr Holbrook?'

However, he said it without any sort of officious manner and dismissed his gendarmes with a gesture.

Despite the closing of the double doors he lowered his voice to little more than a whisper. 'Mr Holbrook, Professor Westgate, I am aware of who you really are. Duvalier put me on to it, mentioning your recent arrival and telling me that he had thought that he recognised your faces but could not remember where he had seen you before. Then, when you had taken to your room he had remembered that he had seen your likenesses in *The Strand*. However, he expressed to me the belief that these likenesses were coincidental and that the shortsighted gentleman and the absent-minded professor could not possibly be Sherlock Holmes and Dr Watson! I agreed that he was doubtless wrong, but now I am sure that you are the famous detective and his Boswell.'

Holmes asked, quietly, 'What has caused you to be so sure?'

'Your diplomatic letters are signed by one "Mycroft Holmes"!'

'So, you have heard of him too?'

'I have read your adventure with the Greek Interpreter.'

I suddenly realised that no matter that we were Sherlock Holmes and Dr Watson, this had not made us the breakers of law or disturbers of the peace. I said, 'Inspector, I believe that you are of too high a rank to be enquiring about incorrect names in a hotel register?'

He laughed pleasantly enough and said, 'Gentlemen, I realise that you are here upon an errand for Her Majesty and do not wish to interfere with this in any way. Indeed it is nothing to do with your affairs that has brought Phillipe to the Splendide. Let me explain; a certain titled French lady, a permanent resident of the hotel, has lost her valuable pearl necklace. We are making a routine search, but I feel quite sure that we will not find the pearls anywhere. We are even stopping guests leaving the building for a quick search of their clothing and any handbags or luggage they may carry. Possibly the bird had flown before we got here, though I somehow doubt it. But if I fail to find the necklace I believe that you will find it for me, Mr Sherlock Holmes!'

My friend asked, 'What makes you say that?'

'Because you are qualified to find it, or so your reputation would suggest. Also I feel that fate has sent you to me, dealt me the card which I have long awaited in my desire for promotion. If you agree to help me I will keep your names out of the matter and take all the glory myself if you succeed. If you refuse I will make it known who you are, and this will spoil your plans, I feel.'

He smiled sweetly and Holmes responded with a sigh, 'You know, Inspector, you are the second blackmailer that I have had to deal with in the space of a few days. I will mention no names in this respect, now or ever, but it rankles, sir, it rankles. However, I will attempt to solve your problem, Inspector, if only because it seems a very elementary one when compared to many that I have been faced with.'

'Elementary, you say; the theft of an extremely valuable pearl necklace?'

'Certainly, if you break the matter down to its elements it will become easier to solve the problem. Let us now consider what has happened . . .'

The inspector muttered to himself in French and then returned to conversing in English. 'Mr Holmes, we have already covered that ground.'

Holmes sat upon one of the huge cushions which served as chairs and, accepting a cigarette of black tobacco from the inspector, which he lit, savoured its smoke.

'A valuable object has, as you say, been purloined. All suspects or even those all but beyond suspicion have been searched, likewise their apartments and luggage. A guard has been placed upon all the entrances and egresses to search all persons who wish to leave. So the problem becomes a simpler one: how is the thief expecting to remove the necklace from these premises, and how has he or she hidden them from your efficient body of gendarmes? The theft is a planned one, I believe.'

I asked, 'What makes you think that particularly?'

'Because, Watson, if it were not, I believe the whole matter would have been already resolved. This is no spur-of-the-moment theft. What we should be looking for is some other unusual happening which might connect with our problem.'

The police inspector breathed hard, not exactly with impatience but with something approaching it. He said, 'Nothing here is unusual, Mr Holmes; this hotel is a splendid one, as its name indicates, with everything moving like clockwork and showing little variance from day to day. The accommodation is good, with a staff of trusted employees who have for the most part been here for years. The cuisine is second to none, with a chef and catering staff beyond reproach.'

'You are going to tell me that these people too have been with the hotel for years?'

'That is so; the chef has recently joined the staff, the old one having retired. But he too is a top-flight professional, well paid and surely beyond suspicion.'

'Is the new chef popular with the rest of the staff?'

'Certainly, Duvalier tells me in fact that he has an understanding with the principal chambermaid, she who must be answered to by the others. They plan to marry and open a restaurant here in Tangier. I have sampled his cuisine and I for one will patronise his establishment.'

Sherlock Holmes, I could tell, needed now the seclusion required to allow him to consider the problem in depth. I knew this mood from my long association with him and attempted to hasten the passing of our guests.

'Inspector, I feel if you were to continue your investigations, following their present line, my friend will have an opportunity to dwell upon the problem.'

The inspector took the hint. 'Certainly. Well, I will meet you at dinner, no doubt. I am fortunate in that tonight the chef presents oysters, of which I am most fond. I do not remember him serving oysters before, but they will, I feel sure, be as perfect as his stews and roasts and *fruites de mer*!

Holmes raised a finger but said nothing as the policemen departed, yet as their footsteps grew less audible he did not sink into one of those reveries of his that I had half expected. Instead he said, 'Watson, could the problem be quite so easy to solve? Upon my word, if we solve this tonight you will be able to chronicle it as my simplest case ever! The inspector is not a dullard; he is, I imagine, as efficient as our old friend Lestrade. Indeed it may be that they both have in common an inability to see that which stares them in the face. We have been press-ganged into this matter, Watson, but must make the best of it. Will you, therefore, aid me by making a circular tour of the exterior of the hotel, paying particular attention to the efficiency of the police arrangements?'

I was happy to serve him, yet asking, 'What shall you be doing whilst I am thus employed?'

I had half expected him to say that it was a three-pipe problem, but instead he said, 'I shall interview the woman who has lost the necklace, for I have very few details concerning the circumstances of the theft.'

Descending the stairs I made for the front entrance to find the inspector and two of his men in the lobby. He saluted, and nodded to his men to let me through. Once outside I made a circular assault upon the building, relieved to find that I was challenged at every possible entrance. However, there was one means of egress which did not appear to be covered. It was the kitchen exit at the rear of the building and there appeared to be no guard upon it.

When I drew the attention of this to the inspector, he said, 'No one uses this door as an entrance and any stranger coming through would be noticed by the kitchen staff. No one leaves by that exit save to put out rubbish and kitchen scraps.'

I tried to think what Holmes's next questions and actions would have been. Deciding to be as thorough as possible, I said, 'Perhaps I could suggest that you place a man at this door?'

He shrugged. 'Certainly, but I assume you would have no objection to the guard allowing the kitchen staff to emerge and throw their scraps in the dustbin? You will note that these are all but full, pending a visit from the rubbish collector.'

For the sake of asking another question to justify my existence, I enquired, 'Do you know the hour of the next collection?'

'Why yes, it is at eight this evening, I believe.'

Making ever increasing circles of the building I gained a good idea of the immediate geography of the Hotel Splendide. I little realised at the time that we would later find this activity of use.

A little later I returned to the room to find Holmes already dressed for dinner. He informed me that he had indeed interviewed the lady, a Countess Valeska, who had been deprived of her necklace.

'A Russian noblewoman, Watson, most disturbed by her loss. She cannot understand how the necklace was taken with only her own trusted servant having access to it, or possibly the head chambermaid, who incidentally is also further beyond suspicion than we already believed her to be, for she is a niece of the manager, Duvalier.'

I told Holmes of my activities and to my surprise I found that he was more than interested in my preoccupation with the kitchen door.

'We will make a detective of you yet, Watson, and I can tell you that some sort of pattern is beginning to form in my mind. Make haste to dress for dinner, Watson, they hold it early here. By the way, what time did you say the rubbish man will call?'

'Eight, Holmes.'

'Splendid, I must bear that in mind . . .'

I had no idea why he should find this detail which I had obtained for want of a sensible question to be of interest. We sat with the inspector at dinner as arranged and being French he paid very special attention to the menu presented. Most of the courses were French in origin, but this was to be expected. I am no great lover of French cuisine myself; give me a jolly good steak and kidney pudding any day; but I had to admit that the food had been well prepared and presented. One thing though puzzled me; that the oysters had been taken from their shells and served on a plate with lemon and dressings in a way quite different to that which I would have expected. I remarked upon this to the others.

The inspector agreed with me that it was unusual, though excused it by saying, 'De Vere, the chef, is a law unto himself. If he does something unusual you can be sure there is a good reason for it.'

Holmes remarked, 'It may be unusual, but it is rather as I had expected.'

I thought little of his remark at the time, and as the oysters were excellent I cared little regarding the shells. Then during the short wait which occurred between the oysters and the ice bombe, Holmes arose from his seat and announced that he wished to smoke a pipe, which he could scarcely do at the dinner table. He did not in fact return until his ice bombe was tepid and his coffee was cold!

It seemed a long time before Holmes returned, but I suppose it was only a matter of about fifteen minutes or so. Then when he did resume his seat and I had poured him a fresh cup of coffee I observed that there was a look of elation about his manner. None the less I reprimanded my friend, 'Your ice bombe is ruined, and the coffee really needs to be replaced with a fresh pot. I trust that your craving for tobacco justifies your missing what was for me the perfect climax to an excellent meal.'

Holmes's eyes twinkled as he replied, 'My dear Watson, the events of the last quarter of an hour would have been worth missing, even for one of Mrs Hudson's meals. Oh, by the way, Inspector, I rather feel that your troubles are over concerning a certain missing article.'

'You mean you have developed a theory concerning the necklace?'

'Rather more than a theory, Inspector. Come, let me give you an account of my activities since I left you for a smoke. At that point I had already formed a theory, but I did not voice it because I felt that it would sound a trifle theatrical; an excellent third act with a brilliant "curtain"! Before I go further I must tell you that both yourself and Watson have played your parts in drawing my mind in the right direction. You see, Inspector, you planted the seed when you mentioned how unusual it was for De Vere to prepare and serve oysters. These seeds were watered by Watson's report of his circuit of the building. He told me that the rubbish collector would call to empty the dustbin at eight of the clock, the actions of putting out and collecting the rubbish evidently to be unsupervised by your gendarmerie. I suppose I should have mentioned this to you, but feared that any change of your plans might scare the birds off so to speak.'

Holmes paused to drink some coffee and to light an Egyptian cigarette. (Really, he has such catholic tastes!) He held our attention, neither the policeman nor I daring to break the spell. In his own good time Holmes continued, 'Then, when the oysters arrived, served minus their shells, I began to think that I was on the right track. Watson had told me that the refuse man would arrive at about eight. At half past seven I decided to see for myself what would happen.'

There came another of his irritating pauses as he fiddled with his coffee.

'Really this coffee is undrinkable, please call the garçon to bring a fresh pot, Watson, there's a good fellow . . .'

I did as he bade me, but to my relief he did not wait for the fresh coffee before continuing his oration. 'I saw the man purporting to be the rubbish collector arrive and busy himself at the dustbin, all but half an hour early. I called upon your gendarmes to challenge him; fortunately the very officers who had been with you when first we met, and they co-operated with me, searching his person and demanding his credentials. He proved bogus as far as his right to collect the rubbish was concerned but nothing incriminating was found about his person. I then turned my attention to the bin itself. On the top of the usual kitchen rubbish was a paper bag of a fairly substantial nature which contained that which I was seeking, about three dozen oyster shells. I took out one of the shells and noted that it was bereft of its oyster but closed and fixed in that particular with some sort of adhesive. I shook the shell and detected the rattle of a small object within. I opened the shell with my penknife to discover inside it a small pearl!'

The inspector could not restrain his interruption. 'You are going to tell me that each of the other shells yielded a pearl also?'

'Exactly, they were varied in size, but I will wager that together they would thread to form the missing necklace.'

I asked, 'So this was the thief's way of getting the necklace out of the building?'

'Of course, Watson, rather ingenious don't you think?'

But the inspector was still puzzled. 'Why then did his accomplice, the bogus rubbish man, not just collect the complete necklace in a paper bag from the bin?'

Holmes responded, 'The thief could not risk having the complete necklace found upon his person or near where he worked. Before the theft had been discovered he broke the string and hid the pearls, each in an empty oyster shell which he then closed with kitchen adhesive made from the white of an egg. It was all to plan, with his fiancée making the actual theft. Then they worked fast, knowing that perhaps there were only minutes before the theft might be discovered. It suited their purpose that they had both been searched, also his kitchen and her apartment. Their confederate, the bogus rubbish man, could have simply taken the bin. But if suspected he might have got away with the bag of shells when the bin was searched. Aside from all this though I believe these three are, how shall I say, "artistes in crime". They perhaps did it as much for the love of the game as much as for the spoils. Oh, by the way, when your men arrested De Vere and his lady accomplice, he was game to the last, for when shown the shells with the pearls inside he asked, "Where else would you find pearls?" It was pointed out to him that no oyster has yet been considerate enough to produce a pearl already bored through for threading!'

The inspector's face was a study, his expressions had truly run the gamut of changes. He breathed hard and then said, 'Mr Holmes, whilst Dr Watson and I partook of our ice bombes you have not only solved the mystery in theory but proved it and in my absence brought the trio of wrongdoers to justice. You have made me feel quite useless!'

Holmes smiled kindly. 'Inspector, I could not have done any of this without the help of the force that you command. I did tell those worthies that the instructions to seize and arrest came straight from yourself. Time was not on my side so I was forced to do that which you would have done, in your absence. Therefore, as Watson and I wish to remain incognito, your report will make no mention of us, please?'

The inspector rose and saluted. 'As you wish, and we will discuss the matter on the morrow, at the police station at noon?'

We agreed to be there.

CHAPTER FOUR

In Search of Marrafaze

On the following morning we presented ourselves at the gendamerie just a few minutes before noon. We were taken immediately to the inspector's office where he served us with some excellent black coffee. As we sipped at the boiling hot, aromatic beverage he read to us his report of the pearl necklace, lost and found; albeit in pieces. Then he paused before saying, 'That then is my report! I believe that all the details are correct save that no mention is made of yourselves. This is just as I hinted last night and I believe you agreed that it should be so. I just wanted to be sure that you are still of that mind, my friends.'

Holmes nodded. 'We are men of our word, and no advantage could come to any of us if it were any other way. So to my mind you owe us nothing, yet I feel sure that you could be of great help to us in our new roles as Holbrook and Westlake.'

'Anything that it is within my power to do, that is proper for me to, I will be happy to grant.'

'Inspector, I would request that you could aid us in our

forthcoming journey into the Sahara Desert. We can, of course, hire the usual camels and drivers to take us as far as the map shows French territory. But I believe that there are marauding tribesmen that may be encountered. Could we therefore ask that you provide a small armed party to accompany us to the very edge of your legal territory?'

'Yes, and I will do it gladly, plus a native guide who will take you to a point near to where legend tells us is the road to Marrafaze. But my friends you will have to journey far beyond, into that part of the vast Sahara that is not claimed by any power, French, Spanish or African. Please also do not forget that you have to return, and this may be even more difficult.'

The inspector was as good as his word and at first light on the following day we found ourselves with the camels that we had managed to hire, along with their drivers, and four armed policemen, though in a tropical style of uniform and headgear which made them look rather more like explorers than law-keepers. They rode not camels but horses of Arabian appearance, with mules to carry their tents and other equipment. The sergeant was clearly French, but the three others were of doubtful parentage, perhaps part French, part Arabian. As for Holmes and I, we were now clad in our 'sahib' outfits, and on the whole it looked a business-like party.

I had not mounted a camel in more than a decade and those with which we were confronted were of a different variety to those that I had encountered in Afghanistan. I was used to the long-haired Bactrian sort, with its two humps, between which a rider could sit with a degree of safety and comfort. These however were, not unnaturally, the Arabian camels, short coated and single humped, requiring a saddle which was rather like a small elephant howdah. To climb into this was easy enough once the camel had been ordered to kneel. One's problems only began when the camel was back on its feet and moving with that bone-shaking gait which has gained it the title of 'the ship of the desert'. Holmes, to my surprise, seemed less discomforted than I, the experienced camel rider. He seemed quickly to gain a sort of counter movement to that of the camel which made him sway far less than I did. But in any case I think his native curiosity served him well with an alternative to any worry about discomfort. His hawk-like eyes were soon scanning as if anxious not to miss any detail of the terrain. We were heading first for Bechar, which we could in fact have reached by train, but these first few hundred miles of camel trek were intended to harden us for the trek through the deep Sahara which would follow.

We avoided towns of any size and preferred to raise our tents beside the oasis which mercifully occurred every so often. But the sergeant, one Pierre Le Roy, warned us, 'When you get to the deep Sahara you will go hundreds of miles before reaching such a heavenly diversion. Even then you will find possibly some resentment from tribesmen who claim these green spots as their own. Remember, we will not be there to protect you with our modern rifles.'

I showed him my own rifle, purchased for the expedition, and my service revolver and pointed out that our Arab camel drivers were armed with rifles.

He laughed, though not with derision. 'Professor, what you have may serve you well, but do not rely too much upon your Arab boys who may desert you or even change sides if you are attacked by tribesmen. You will notice that they carry weapons which are more like muskets than rifles and fire a single shot when loaded. As for myself and my party, I will take you well beyond French territory and well on the road to the fabled Marrafaze, if it exists. I can but point you to where explorers have told it lies. Before that we will travel many hundreds of miles. Before the end of our journey together I will try to hire fresh guides and camels, for these will turn back at a certain point.'

Holmes keenly enquired, 'From fear or fatigue?'

The sergeant laughed. 'A little of each; these are primitive people you have hired, sir, and they believe that at that point in the Sahara which is beyond their knowledge the world itself ends. To them the world is flat with a danger that if their camels bolted they might be propelled into limitless space. You will need guides from just beyond the "known world", who are aware that this is not so.'

Holmes and I discussed the sergeant's advice later and Holmes felt that he was a man to be depended upon. 'He is brave enough to stray into unknown territory to aid us. Mark you, he would possibly prefer to lengthen his expedition with us than make an early return to the tedium of his duties in Tangier. However, I must not be cynical in my thoughts of him, for he has given us the most honest advice yet.'

It took us many days to reach Bechar, by which time we had gained a little experience of the more intensive desert travel to come, but this did not prevent us enjoying a brief respite when we stayed the night in a hotel, which was adequate, though not of the quality of Tangier's Splendide.

Whilst there we met several quite unusual people, one of whom seemed interested in our travels. He was an Arab of expansive build, wearing European clothing but wearing a tarbush upon his head. He had a rather furtive manner, hinting that he seemed to know something of the purpose of our mission. Fortunately he was quite mistaken in his assumptions. 'Honoured Efendim, not many Englishmen who are not soldiers are seen this far toward the deep Sahara. Could it be that you are seeking the lost city of gold which is believed to exist just beyond where the ignorant think the world ends?'

Holmes gave me a guiding line when he replied, 'Sir, we are archaeologists: our interest is in prehistoric remains rather than gold. We seek tombs which we believe will pre-date those of the Egyptian Pharoahs.'

Our new friend insisted on buying arrack for us all and then wagged a finger of disbelief.

I said, 'You do not then believe in even the possibility of such tombs?'

'Not really, Efendi, the stories about them come from the same sort of people who believe in a legendary land which they call Marrafaze.'

He took us out to the edge of the desert, pointing toward where the mythical tombs were supposed to exist. Then he pointed slightly to the south and remarked that Marrafaze was supposed to be in that direction. But then he gave his own opinion of these suppositions by saying, 'Go either way, and you will find nothing but hundreds of miles of sand under a sun that will scorch relentlessly.'

When the time came for us to recommence our journey, Holmes indicated to Sergeant Le Roy the direction of the fabled tombs rather than that of the legendary land we were seeking.

'If observed, Sergeant, I want it to appear that we do not seek Marrafaze. Possibly we could then change direction once out of the range of even those powerful field glasses owned by the Arab at the hotel.'

I had not seen any field glasses, and asked how he could know that the man owned such optical aids.

'My dear Westlake, the fellow wore a sports shirt, open at the neck, minus cravat. Did you not observe the scar made by a thin cord about his fleshy neck? I cannot think of any other object that he would hang around his neck regularly enough to make such a trench in his flesh. In fact if you look back you will see the flash of the twin lenses against the sun!'

I looked back and surely, there on the hotel balcony, stood the fat Arab, following our departure through field glasses. He waved, and we waved back and our little caravan did not veer in direction until it would have been impossible for him to observe us even with artificial aids to the vision.

For the next four days we travelled, fairly uneventfully, coming across no other travellers or wild beasts, and precious few oases. We were making for one of these, known to Le Roy fortunately. The heat from the sun was indeed relentless, and we soon in fact changed to travelling in the cool of the evening and making faster headway. Then, just as our water supply was dangerously low, we spotted the haven to which Le Roy was leading, the oasis of Wadi el Hazier. The sergeant evidently knew it of old and that we were free to drink from its wells and eat of its dates. The latter made a pleasant change from our tinned bully and ship's biscuits. The asses were watered before anything else was done, for unlike the camels they did not carry their own emergency supply. Then when the camels had been refreshed we sat beneath the date palms, blessing their heavenly shade and fruitful bounty. After twenty-four hours of blessed lassitude, Le Roy and his party made ready to leave us. As they loaded their asses with dates for the return journey he showed us the way we should go.

'Gentlemen, if you follow your compass due south for another four days it is my belief that you will find the land of Marrafaze. As it is not on any map I cannot be certain, but I have done the best I can for you. We are already in uncharted territory so really you are on your own. Try to chart your return journey as you go. God be with you, and keep a sharp eye on your Arabs!'

The departure of the French party gave me a slight sinking feeling in my stomach, but I observed no dismay in the manner of my friend. Moreover, the Arabs showed no sign of giving us any trouble, and the camels seemingly refreshed by their break were making good time. The first day we covered some thirty-five miles by our reckoning, which from the experience of recent days seemed quite respectable. However, we had to remember that we had no map so had no idea as to how far we would travel before finding water. Holmes was, however, optimistic, saying, 'Abdul travelled out of the land we seek; I feel sure therefore that periodic oases must exist.'

But after travelling for three days, some hundred miles perhaps, we had not encountered or even distantly sighted any shade or water. Holmes still presented his jaunty exterior but I knew him well enough to know that this was for my benefit, and that of the Arabs. Indeed at the end of a further day, during which our rate of progress began to slow down, even my friend was beginning to lose his air of optimism.

Then came the morning when we emerged from our tent to find that the Arabs had deserted us, having stolen away silently in the night as only people of those desert regions can. Holmes was doubtless as dismayed as I, but was as essentially practical as ever.

'So much for the inspector's choice of guides, Watson! Ah well, let us make a balance sheet of what our assets may be, if any!'

I quickly remarked, 'They have left us two camels and an ass at least.'

'How kind of them! They only left us those because I fixed their long lead ropes to the pole inside our tent and even the Arabs might have disturbed us if they had come close enough to interfere with these. I had feared something like this might happen, Watson; all the signs were there. Our guides either doubted the existence of Marrafaze, or else knew that it was too far for us to reach it. Let us hope that the former is correct.'

'If you suspected this catastrophe, Holmes, why did you not inform me?'

'Because, Watson, you would have been heroic and might have got us both killed. Better they steal away than shoot us as we slept, which they might well have done had they thought we suspected their intended desertion. Well, at least we have camels and an ass to carry our tent and other articles. It will be a harsh journey but given a little luck we will survive. It is in our favour that we do at least know that Marrafaze exists and that our direction is the right one. Aside from this the likelihood of our encountering an oasis if we travel another day or so is an encouraging one. Now let us start to be sensible and prepare for a day's journey.'

It fell out that we had a large goatskin of water, enough to keep us alive for several days, and the Arabs had left us a few dates and tins of beans and bully. We had two rifles, which fortunately had been beside us as we slept, and my service revolver which I had not let far from my sight since the journey had started. I knew from my war experiences that the camels could go for several more days without water and might even survive as long without food. But the ass was a different matter and would need at least to drink before long. However, we fixed the tent and equipment onto the poor beast and saddled our camels. I had learned the commands to make them kneel so that we could saddle them, and made them rise so that I could strap their girths: then I made them kneel again that we might mount. They were amiable enough beasts, fortunately. (The reader will know what I mean if he has any experience of 'the ship of the desert'. These animals, unlike a horse, can kick in any direction and if annoyed can direct their saliva into one's face with a deadly aim. But these two were docile — and we treated them with respect.)

As I had performed these menial tasks, Holmes had stood, smoking a pipe and gazing into the far distance. I had not remonstrated with him for not assisting me, for I knew that he was using his brilliant mind to just about the best purpose that he could put it to: our survival. But he mounted his camel with alacrity and as I shouted 'Hut,

hut!' the two strangely graceful creatures carried us forward willingly enough, with the ass trailing with rather less enthusiasm.

We made rather fewer miles than we had on previous days because the heat from the sun seemed to be getting more and more relentless. We were grateful for our hats and tropical clothing and we had to use all our will power regarding our water supply. Eventually we pitched our tent, if a trifle carelessly, having completed no more than a score of miles, if that. The camels seemed grateful to be unsaddled again and sank onto their knees without needing to be so bidden. I unloaded the ass and realised that it was in a really terrible condition. As it rested I doubted it would even get up again, let alone be able to carry anything. After we had eaten a few dates, biscuits and a slice of bully we gratefully drank a cup of water each and held a 'council of war'.

I began this by saying, 'Holmes, I have had experience with camels and asses as you know. Please accept my judgement that the ass will not carry our goods further, and I doubt it will live another day without water. May I suggest that I take my revolver and put the poor creature out of its misery this very night?'

Holmes shook his head. 'I am for delaying such a drastic step, Watson, for I have noticed certain signs about the desert that lead me to become slightly more optimistic about our future. I will not detail these because I do not wish to raise false hopes. Enough to say that I suggest we load the camels with the equipment tomorrow, ourselves walking beside them and leading the ass, unladen, in which state he may stumble a few more miles. We may find water before he reaches expiry.'

At this point I noticed that the groundsheet upon which we usually lay was missing. I remembered laying it and remarked upon this. But Holmes dismissed the subject saying, 'Perhaps it slipped your mind, the sun and heat play tricks with the brain, Watson; spread your jacket and sleep upon it.'

Although I knew that I had laid the sheet I had not the strength to argue and being much fatigued soon fell into a deep sleep.

When I awoke I noted that Holmes was already outside the tent and was standing, observing the ass, which stood, if a little unsteadily, upon its legs. I was surprised, for I had half expected it to expire during the night. It was licking at tiny amounts of puddled water which were upon the groundsheet which was spread upon the sand, or rather laid into a shallow trench. I then realised what the shrewd Sherlock Holmes had done, having made a kind of shallow dish of the waterproofed cloth to catch the dew. The ass had licked up most of it and it was soon again without moisture. But tiny as the amount of water had been, its effect upon the animal was at least noticeable.

'Come, Watson, we will load the camels as quickly as we can. As for Neddy here, I have plans for him now that he can walk a little.'

I knew better than to press my friend for details, which he would doubtless reveal in his own good time. Instead I set to work willingly to prepare the camels for their new role as pack animal rather than steeds. Soon we were on our way with myself leading the camels and Holmes unaccountably leading the unladen ass. In fact he even had the animal taking the lead and actually pulling at the rope upon which he held it. After a mile or two Holmes stopped us and suggested that I drive a stake at which to tether the camels, which I did, though somewhat puzzled.

'Come, Watson, we will give Neddy his head now. He has not the strength to bolt and we can easily keep up with him. By the way, bring the shovel.'

I took the shovel from the back of one of the camels and followed as Holmes dropped the rope to release the ass. The camels were grateful to rest as we followed the little grey quadruped. As we walked Holmes explained, 'When we travelled yesterday I noticed some very occasional signs of plant life protruding from the sand. Today I have noted that, although sparse, there are slightly more of these.'

I grasped his meaning. 'Where there is any sort of growth there must be at least a hint of water?'

'Exactly, and the more often wisps of prairie grass occur the nearer one is to an oasis proper. Of course it might be two days away yet, and would come too late to save our friend here, but note how distended are his nostrils, Watson. His sense of smell is far greater than ours. With luck he will lead us to water, which may strengthen us all and enable us to reach the oasis which inevitably will appear on the skyline.'

'You mean he can actually smell water?'

'Yes, but I doubt if he can make access to it without our help, hence the shovel that you are carrying.'

He was right, of course, as usual, and the ass followed its nose with its head held alternately high and then near the sand for a further hundred yards or so, before starting to circle in a very strange manner. Then the animal stopped and started to scrape at the sand with its hooves. Eventually the depression it made revealed a hint of dampness in the sand. But the ass had spent the last of its strength and fell to its knees. I at once set to work with a will and within a few minutes had produced a sort of puddle of mud. More effort still and I had transformed the mud to some actual water, though very muddy it was. Soon I had made a tiny oasis of our own in the seemingly merciless desert. The ass struggled to his feet, tottered to the hole I had dug and started to drink, seeming not to care how muddy the liquid was. As I stood and watched him, marvelling at the way he seemed to recover his strength before my very eyes Holmes returned to fetch the camels. Once the donkey had drunk his fill I enlarged the hole still further and the camels drank from it gratefully, even if their need was the least of us all.

When the animals had all had their fill I strained some of the muddy water through a neckerchief into a metal cup and thence into the water bottle which I had noted was extremely low in content.

'Come, Watson, we will continue our journey with rather more confidence, I feel. We must, however, remain alert for signs of the oasis upon which we still depend.'

We did not see those heavenly signs that day, but made camp with every hope of doing so on the morrow. We were now very far into the deep Sahara. We knew how far behind us was the last oasis, and as we probably had little chance of making such a journey, it was a better gamble to go on. Of course there were times when we doubted the wisdom of this philosophy, knowing that we and our animals could not survive for very long on muddy water occasionally unearthed. Water aside, the camels and ass required food urgently, not being able to survive on a share of our own meagre rations which in any case were now down to one tin of bully beef, a handful of biscuits and very little else. We could go on, man and beast, for a day, possibly two. Sighting something more than a mirage became hourly more vital.

'Look, Watson, I believe I can see a patch of green upon the horizon!'

Trust Holmes's eagle eye to spot it, and an oasis for sure, unless we were both seeing the same mirage, which seemed unlikely. Indeed another two hours of steady plodding showed that it was quite a large fertile spot that lay only a few miles ahead of us. The animals were already showing great interest in our goal and willing beasts that they were I believe we would have had great difficulty had we attempted to alter their direction of progress. I offered up a silent prayer of thanks for our deliverance from what could have been the 'Final Problem'!

'We must approach with caution, Watson, for we do not know if this green place is presently inhabited, and if so what the mood of those inhabitants might be.'

Trust Holmes, I thought, to be quite so over-cautious. I said, 'I am so yearning for water, food and shade that I am willing to take a chance.'

Even so we did proceed with caution and eventually arrived at the oasis without seeing any signs of life. There was a well with clean, cool drinking water as well as a pool from which the poor beasts could slake their thirsts. Moreover there were bushes, grass and some date palms and we released the animals that they might browse, being sure that they would not stray from this heavenly spot. The camels nibbled eagerly at the bushes whilst the poor little ass filled himself with various grasses. We had removed all of their saddles and harness and it was good to see them rest when they had eaten and drunk their fill. We could find no food to interest us save the dates from the palms, but we celebrated by eating the last of our supplies of biscuit and bully. We made a kind of stew, having lit a fire, the heat from which we were grateful for as the cool night descended. We sat and smoked our pipes by the fireside, spared even the effort of pitching the tent as there was a rude shelter in which to sleep. I suppose we really should have slept in turn, each taking a spell at watching, but we had reached the stage where we felt that there was not much we could do if attacked.

But we had quite forgotten the possibility of marauding wild beasts, for we had encountered none so far. We had I suppose forgotten that the oasis might attract beast as well as man. We were therefore surprised in the small hours to be awakened by a series of shrill howls. I knew that these, although canine, were not produced by dogs or wolves, and we soon discovered that we had attracted the unwelcome attention of a group of jackals. They had encircled our animals like a swift darting yellow ring, but I knew that the camels at least were safe from them. Indeed these looked upon them with that disdain which is said to adorn their faces because they know the one hundreth name of god. They uttered fearsome roars, almost like those of a lion, and the ass made quite a fearsome vocal display as well.

I drove off the creatures with a lighted brand from the fire and they scattered, only to tentatively return after a few minutes. Then I fired a round from my service revolver and we saw them no more that night. But for safety we put the halters on the camels and the ass and tethered them near to the shelter. After that we each kept watch in turns whilst the other slept.

Came the dawn and the rising sun threatened another searing hot day, making us in no hurry to leave our green haven. We held a council of war and Holmes suggested that we spend the day in collecting dates with which to load the ass, along with our goatskin bottles refilled with clear water.

'Then, Watson, I suggest that we rest a little more today and start to continue our journey as night falls. With the camels now rested and in the cool of the night we could cover quite a lot of ground before we see another dawn.'

I understood what was in his mind; for now speed was more important, as we could not exist entirely on dates for too long. It was vital now that we reach our goal, the legendary land of Marrafaze.

CHAPTER FIVE

The Legend Attained

We were encouraged by sights of other forms of life aside from the jackals as we swayed on camelback by moonlight. This told me that we were getting nearer to some sort of desert edge. Some of the luminous eyes were unnerving until one saw that they only represented the optics of harmless little creatures, such as desert hares, and rats of the gerbil of jerboa varieties, leaping about on kangaroo-like limbs. Then, as the dawn broke we saw a different set of creatures such as ostrich and onager, which is a wild ass of a size to make our Neddy look like a seaside donkey.

I was somewhat surprised to see the ostriches, and ventured to remark to Holmes that I had believed them extinct in these regions. Holmes, however, was in no mood for ornithological discussion, and remarked rather curtly that perhaps I should claim them as an entirely new sub-species, *Struthiornidae Watsonii*! His sense of humour is occasionally of the oddest; rather hurt, I refrained from further comment, but the sight of those great birds reinforced the sense of unreality which had come over me. We were indeed now in territory quite unknown to any Western explorer.

Then, as I was scanning the horizon for some sign of a habitation I espied a cloud of dust which could only be made by the hooves of quite a number of animals. I pointed it out to Holmes who showed no great surprise. 'I have been observing it for some minutes, Watson. I rather fancy we will before long encounter a party of riders.'

'Not a herd of onager or a group of ostrich?'

'I think not, for those we have encountered were not travelling at such speed or in a straight formation. No, these are horses, probably ridden by Bedouin tribesmen. Well, Watson, they could well be friendly, but so far into uncharted territory, who can say?'

Soon the clouds of dust could be made out to be indeed horsemen, and as the dust clouds lessened we assumed this meant they were slowing down, having observed us perhaps with apprehension. A few minutes more and we could see that there were perhaps a score of riders in Arab robes, their steeds being typical small Arab horses. One of their number was making for us as the rest of them slowed down a little. This single advance guard turned out to be bearded, swarthy and armed to the teeth. He had a musket on his shoulder and in his belt a flintlock pistol of the kind that I had only previously encountered in museums or private collections. Its handle was bejewelled and his musket appeared so decorated too, whilst in his right hand he brandished an extremely businesslike-looking sabre. I was dismayed by what we could see of his arms and attitude. We stopped our camels and I took the hint from Holmes as he sat tall in his ungainly saddle, his great beak of a nose projecting as he stared at the newcomer in a most wide-awake manner.

The Bedouin reined his horse and surveyed us for perhaps twenty seconds before making a salaam which we returned. Then he spoke in a form of Arabic, or what seemed so, of which we had not even a beginner's knowledge. I tried my few words in the more usual form of the language without making much headway. Then Holmes thought to address him in French, which he responded to with a quaint old-world version of that language.

Holmes greeted him politely but firmly. 'Honoured sir, we are glad to see you. We seek the legendary Sheikdom of Marrafaze. Perhaps you know of it and can direct us. If you have food to spare we would give you money, Arabian or European, in exchange.'

The Arab said, 'Show me this coinage of which you speak.'

We showed him examples of the various coinages that we carried but he seemed singularly unimpressed. 'Those discs of inferior metal are no use to us, but we will exchange some flour, meat and such things for your camels.'

We politely declined his offer but I noticed with concern that the other similarly mounted and armed Arabs had made a circle around us. I fingered the handle of my revolver but Holmes spoke to me quietly in English. 'No, Watson, they are heavily armed and even with those antique weapons they would soon make mincemeat of us. With luck we might retain our weapons and a few other things.'

He proved to be right as they led away our camels after we had dismounted but showed little interest in anything else we carried. Their spokesman made another oration. 'You may keep that sad excuse for a donkey and that refuse which it carries. Here is a bag of flour, some dried goat and some figs. Take them and be on your way.'

We both knew that there was nothing which we could do that might control the situation; we were fortunate that the bandit Bedouin (for how else could you describe them) had not taken our lives as well as our camels. At least they had left us a tent, two rifles and various other articles, plus the ass to carry them. Moreover they had given us some provisions, though I doubt if they were a fair exchange for two camels and their harnesses and howdah-like saddles. I decided that we had little to lose by asking them about our goal. 'Could you tell us how far is Marrafaze?'

The Bedouin leader laughed hugely. 'Marrafaze? Efendi, you have to reach the end of the world before you can even consider finding it. I have never been there myself, but I wish you good luck if that is where you want to go. I suggest that you drink deeply, for there are few oases between this one and the end of the world.'

I asked the obvious question. 'What form does it take, this end of the world?'

'You will possibly find out, Efendi, if you survive to see it.'

Then with a 'Hut, hut, hut' these rascals departed, taking our camels with them. Soon they were only a distant cloud of dust. Holmes had spoken not at all for some time and I wondered what were his thoughts, asking, 'What do you make of this end-of-the-world business, Holmes?'

He answered in a very subdued manner. 'It has been

mentioned to us before and I have noticed that the Arabs are reluctant to dwell upon it as a subject. But I would imagine that it is some kind of natural barrier which by its very nature would suggest the world's end to primitive people. Perhaps it is the edge of a huge lake which they cannot navigate or a sheer cliff which they cannot climb. But as our friend the bandit sheik remarked, if we survive we will find it. We will make a start at sunset.'

'How about the jackals, or other beasts?'

'I think, Watson, they present less of a threat than does the heat of the sun. Now I suggest we start to gather together everything that the ass can carry and anything else that we can manage ourselves.'

We lost no time in deciding what we could take and what we could not. The tent was essential for shade or protection from sudden sand storms, and this, plus cooking equipment and some ammunition we would load, we decided, upon the poor, willing beast. Extra clothing and things of that sort we loaded into canvas bags to carry on our own backs. Indeed, our own loads grew heavier and more ungainly as each fresh essential was decided upon. We encouraged the ass to eat of the foliage as much as possible, but Holmes decided that we would need to take a feed or two for Neddy.

'Note that which he eats, Watson, and cut with the sabre as much as you can. Meanwhile I will try to gather some more dates.'

He was as good as his word, shinning up a tree with amazing agility for a man of middle years. As I hacked at the grasses I was interrupted at regular intervals by the thudding upon the ground of large branches of dates. Later

I began to wonder how we would carry these things, but Holmes had a plan.

'Watson, we will make a cart which the ass will pull, loaded with the sustenance that will support both him and us.'

'Do you think we could make such a thing? I mean how about the wheels?'

'It will take the form of a sledge, Watson, and there is no time to lose.'

We did indeed fashion a sort of cart, from pieces of aged wood which we found around the oasis, bound together with all the cords and rope we could spare, plus a few lengths of pliable vine-like plants of the convulvulus variety which abounded. It was no thing of beauty and joy forever, but we considered that the ass would be able to pull it without too much difficulty. As for ourselves, we would have to walk, perhaps a long way, indeed to 'the end of the world'!

We started off bravely enough, getting through an entire period of darkness with seeing more than a few rodents and the odd jackal, which gave us no problems. We seemed to make quite good progress, though by dawn had covered nowhere near as far as we would have with the camels. Then we put up the tent and we got what little shade it could afford us. I unloaded the ass so that he could have a roll and a rest, whilst Holmes made breakfast. He made some sort of pancakes from flour and water which he cooked over a small fire in the frying pan. We ate these with some dates and made some coffee which went down well. Our main thought was to get these domestic tasks finished before the midday sun should make every movement a great effort. We slept fitfully, for perhaps four hours, by which time the heat was growing less unbearable. I would have much liked a wash, but we had not enough water. We ate a few dates and I gave Neddy some of the greenery that he had pulled behind him. I had no water for the poor beast but hoped that we would find another oasis within a day or so.

For three more days and nights we continued in this way until we started to feel the strain of our situation. We had fancied we might perhaps be travelling in the direction of a less arid terrain, but the opposite seemed to be the truth. We tried letting the ass have his head, a procedure which had found water for us once before, but he showed little interest, which illustrated either his failing strength or the absence of the moisture itself. But we did have one stroke of good fortune in the discovery by Holmes of an ostrich egg. With this and some flour we were able to make proper pancakes, after an hour of trying to open the huge egg. Eventually Holmes blew a large hole in its seemingly impenetrable shell with his rifle. We were able to pour out the contents, which were fortunately reasonably fresh.

The day dawned when I debated the kindness of shooting the ass, which was clearly dying of hunger and thirst. He had served us well and I did not wish him to suffer. But then the miracle occurred which saved his life, and possibly our own. (For who knows how far we could have struggled on without a beast of burden?) It rained; and when I say that I know that anyone who has ventured onto the African continent will believe me when I say that the heavens opened.

We put down every sort of bowl, basin or waterproof cloth that we boasted to catch the wonderful life-giving droplets. Soon there was enough to make the ass like a different animal. We had hastily raised the tent and needed to shelter beneath its waterproof canvas for several days. But then after the second day of drenching downpour it started to reduce its ferocity and we were able to continue on our way. As the rain decreased until it was more like an English summer shower we started to make better time again, and after a further day it all but stopped and we noticed that the desert was becoming almost fertile with small red flowers and brave blades of grass at intervals. These helped us little save in providing at least a decent snack for the ass. Then as if Mother Nature was trying to make our tribulations up to us, she presented us with an oasis: a small one, but a welcome sight it was. It was just a natural pool which could well have been arid before the rain but was now quite a respectable little watering hole. There was no shelter or even any sign that anyone had been there before us; no tracks, save those of desert creatures. But there was shade, welcome now that the sun was so strong again, and we were able to gather our strength and eat the last of our provisions. (Save for flour which we still had quite a lot of.) There were shrubs for the ass, but no dates upon the palms which were extremely stunted. Holmes decided that it was an entirely natural oasis, possibly never visited by man before.

'Come, Watson, can you see any sign of even the most primitive attempts to take advantage of this pool? No one has tried to build a well in order to conserve the periodic surplus of water. Why, there is not even a rude shelter. If a party like the Arabs that we encountered had been here, even many years ago, they would have left some sign or clue that they had been here. No, this small green place fills me with optimism, and not just because it has probably saved our lives.'

'Then why, Holmes?'

'Why, I'll tell you why . . . because it is near the end of the world!'

Anyone else, anyone who had not been with us during the preceding weeks would have thought that the sage of Baker Street was losing his once remarkable intellect. But I knew at once that he was referring to that mythical place of which we had heard rumour.

'You think we could be nearing it?'

'I am sure we are.'

'What deductions have I missed?'

I was bearded, dirty, my skin plentifully layered in sand, my throat was dry with weeks of the desert. Baker Street, and my friend's 'methods' and deductions seemed to me now to be part of a very distant past. We had little left to eat or drink and all that we had was contained in two back-sacks and on the back of an ass that might, thanks to the little pond, recover his strength and spirit. That Holmes could still think about deductions seemed incredible. I supposed he might keep his optimism as long as his tobacco held out!

I think he sensed my feelings and he rounded on me with a will. 'Watson, you must buck up. For the moment we have water and enough food to ensure that we survive for another day. Come, we will take water from the pool with which to wash and shave. Then we will change our clothes and continue on to the end of the world.'

'What form do you really think it will take?'

'I am expecting to find, no more than twenty miles from here, an incline ending in a sort of cliff's edge or bluff. What lies beyond we cannot say, but obviously it is a considerable deterrent to progress. I expect there to be an unusual weather manifestation, such as a dense, permanent fog.'

This was indeed the old Sherlock Holmes speaking but I could not see how he could deduce any of these things.

'What makes you believe that we are getting near to whatever it is that we shall find, or that it will take the form of a cliff or bluff?'

'Watson, have you studied your own footprints lately, or mine for that matter?'

'Why no, but then I cannot imagine why I should do so.'

'If you had done so you would have noticed that we are now walking upon the mildest of slopes, even where there has been no shifting of the sand. Your toecaps are sinking further forward than when you were walking on flat ground. In other words we are going almost imperceptibly uphill. If this tendency increases at its present rate we will shortly come upon an actual hill, or sharp rise of some kind.'

'Could it then not simply slope downward upon the side beyond its apex?'

'That is not impossible, but I feel that it is more than a hill; more likely a high ridge stretching for a great many miles, a sort of natural barrier. Primitive people might be forgiven for thinking it to be the end of the world.'

I was still a little doubtful. 'Why would they think this, however simple their philosophy? After all, we know that the world is round, so there must be something beyond such a ridge; perhaps a lake, or some distant vistas of more desert or other terrain.'

'That would be true if such could be seen; but the fact that it evidently cannot leads me to believe in some kind of natural phenomenon hiding what is beyond from view; perhaps a vapour or mist.'

He decided that once we were refreshed and rested we would continue on foot without the ass and equipment. Holmes planned to leave our equine friend at the oasis, without any sort of harness or restraint. We would, he planned, pack just our necessities into our back packs and in that way cover the ground much faster.

My concern was immediately for Neddy. 'You mean to abandon him here?'

'Watson, we are leaving him with plenty of water and foliage. Without the effort of carrying our equipment he will quickly recover and will eventually seek pastures new. Instinct will take him in the right direction and unhampered he will cover the ground quickly, just as we will. The only alternative is to put your revolver to his head. But I think to free him will give him a fair chance of survival. If we find nothing in two days we will return here and chances are he will still be in the vicinity.'

His words made sense and I confess my agreement with them was partly due to a dislike of the idea of shooting the poor beast. As it was, the ass showed little concern at our departure, being too happy with his complete lack of harness. I knew that the water and what foliage there was would be enough to restore his health and strength.

Our progress, as Holmes had predicted, was rapid compared with that which we had made when having to match our pace to that of the heavily loaded beast. We took what food we had, full carafes of water and the rifles. We also each had a blanket in our back packs in which to survive the cold desert nights. The first day we covered twenty miles or so, a rate that I doubted we would be able to maintain. (For we were presently refreshed and rested.) By the time we made a rude shelter with the blankets we had already noted that the slope was now distinct.

By the time I emerged from beneath the blankets Holmes had made us a primitive breakfast from flour and water over a small fire that he had managed. Ironic to the end, he remarked, 'Late for breakfast as ever, Watson. Come, I am already finished and contemplating the day over a cup of coffee. Get the fritter down you, my dear fellow, you will find it contains the odd fig fragment and slice of date.'

I was hungry enough for Holmes's concoction to go down quite well and I taxed him for an idea of his plans for the day.

He considered. 'I believe that by nightfall we will reach the end of the world, given that we make good time again. Just how close to Marrafaze that might bring us is indeed hard to tell. Friend Abdul might have given us more information than he did. The fault is mine for I took in all he said about the remoteness of our goal, but had wrongly assumed that we would be guided the whole way. But so far we have done well, Watson, we have done well indeed. Be of good cheer, we may soon be handing our credentials to the Sheik!'

He was right about the increasing sharpness of the slope and by midday, when we rested and shaded ourselves from the sun, we were actually walking uphill. By our next pause, as the sun went down, we were finding the incline quite hard going. Then, just when the great orange sphere seemed about to disappear in the west, I spotted what I took to be an oasis upon the horizon.

However, Holmes disagreed with me. 'You see, Watson, what appears to you to be the tops of some date palms actually continues for a great distance to both east and west. I think that is the edge of the bluff that I predicted. However, I fear we must wait until dawn to find out, for we will not reach it before dark. Another mile or two and we must stop for a few hours' sleep. Should we continue in the dark we could well fall over the edge!'

We made a few more miles until we could no longer make out the ridge of green, and I confess that when we stopped I was too excited by the thoughts of what we might find for slumber. Holmes, however, was soon in the arms of Morpheus.

It was my turn therefore to be the early riser and I tried to get some kind of breakfast going. There was practically nothing left, save a handful of flour and some Fry's cocoa grains in the bottom of a tin. I mixed these together with some water and tried to imitate Holmes's miraculous way of producing a pancake or fritter. We were hungry enough for these to go down well and they were too quickly finished.

'Just think, Watson, if we had brought the ass we could have had some meat. Wince if you must, but I'll wager that if we do not quickly find food your repugnance at such an idea will daily decrease!'

This repulsive suggestion at least allayed my hunger. I said, 'Come, let us put such horrific thoughts from our minds and see if we have reached the end of the world.'

We grew nearer to the greenery and as we stopped for the midday sun, Holmes cautioned me. 'Watson, we must tread carefully from this point. We may even at this very moment be standing upon a portion of unsafe land, jutting out above a chasm. When we start again we must take a step at a time to make sure of our safety.'

I believe the best way to describe that which we encountered is to remind the reader of some of those crumbling cliffs of chalk upon the south coast of Britain. One can in some cases go uphill to their edges, only to be standing on an overhang of an unsafe nature. This cliff was, of course, of sandstone, but just as brittle. Further, whilst at Dover or Eastbourne one can see from the edge just how far down is the sea, at 'the end of the world' one could see only a few yards downward through the formation of a sort of fog-like vapour. The sun produced an eerie yet beautiful effect as it shone down to give the appearance of a steamy rainbow. I remarked upon its beauty, but Holmes was unimpressed.

'Watson, beauty often hides the viper's sting, and in this case the danger is very real. One can so easily understand why the Bedouin consider this to be the end, or perhaps the edge, of the world. Who knows what they believe to be lurking beneath those deceptive clouds?'

'How far down do you think we can expect to find solid land?'

'I am not a mathematician, Watson, but I have an idea that it must be more than a quarter of a mile! I calculated this from the degree that the land inclined from where it ceased to be flat. As I walked beside you I was not wasting my time.'

'It will not then be possible for us to descend, given such a distance and lack of visibility.'

'Nonsense, Watson. Abdul has done so more than once.'

Gingerly we investigated, lying full length and leaning our heads over the edge. We were looking for a place where there was no overhang, where there might be a fairly straight sandstone cliff face. We found such a place at last.

'There is danger in it, Watson, for we have no rope. Do you still have the tent-pegs in your haversack?'

I found that I had some of these which I had forgotten to leave behind with the tent. They were metal skewers, about fourteen inches in length, but I had no hammer with which to drive them. However, I reckoned that I could knock them easily enough into the soft sandstone with the butt of my service revolver. But we needed some sort of rope to make a safety line. Eventually we took the belts from our tunics, made them into loops which could be engaged upon a tent peg. Our plan was this: we would each take half a dozen tent pegs in addition to that which supported the belt. We could lean over and drive this in first, then another peg as far below as we could reach. The idea was to make a ladder to descend, removing and replacing the pegs as we descended. For additional safety we would have one arm inside the belt loop, the peg of which we would also need to move on the way down. It was a highly dangerous enterprise, given the fragility of the sandy rock and the weight of ourselves and our rifles, which we considered we should not sacrifice. We discussed it at some length.

'Do you think we can do it, Holmes?'

'I have done it in the Alps, though with proper pegs and safety lines, but in principle it will work.'

'How far down must we go before we know how deep the drop could be?'

'Impossible to say, Watson though I would guess that we would quickly find ourselves below the vapour. On the credit side, we might even find ledges on the descent, even small caves. There may not be land below; it could be water, some vast lake or even yet a volcanic interior.'

'You mean we could be climbing down into the interior of a volcano?'

'I think it is possible. Please remember, Watson, we do not have to make the descent.'

I thought carefully before I replied, 'What then is the alternative?'

Holmes's eyes twinkled as he said, 'We could retrace our footsteps and walk several hundred miles without camels or the ass and with most of our equipment gone, with our water and food all but gone.'

'We would never survive!'

'We might!'

'Is there more chance of survival through turning ourselves into mountaineers?'

'I believe so.'

'Then the chance is worth taking.'

We agreed on this then, and made an almost immediate start.

CHAPTER SIX

Descent from the Edge of the World

I have described to the reader the manner of our intended descent but I cannot really describe the abject terror with which I faced it. Maybe Sherlock Holmes was going through a similar stark terror, but if he was he showed no sign of it. As we talked, his voice was clear and without that tremor which I feel sure my own must have betrayed. Holmes made the first move and had soon proved the practicality of what we had devised. I followed him, after some moments of hesitation.

'Steady, Watson, no hurry, my dear fellow!'

I feel sure that my friend's calming voice saved my life each time I faltered. I tried to concentrate on what I was doing and at the same time think of a foggy day in Baker Street and other nostalgic pleasures. As it happened the very vapour through which we descended was a help to my confidence, for there was no point in looking downward even if I wished to. Quite soon the sun was shining down, through the vapour rather than down onto it, and the fog itself was not making it easier for us to breathe.

Eventually there came a heavenly break from our dangerous descent when Holmes's feet found themselves firmly planted upon a quite considerable ledge. We collapsed onto this and tried to regain our wits and confidence. The ledge was perhaps six feet deep in places and felt fairly secure. We sat there with our backs to the cliff and soon Holmes was smoking a pipe of his dwindling stock of tobacco.

'Watson, we have proved that it can be done. I perceive moreover that the vapour is thinning below us and we should soon be able to get some idea of the enormity of our task.'

Eventually we descended again by our proven method and to our joy, after perhaps a quarter of an hour, we discovered another, even deeper, ledge. We walked upon this more boldly and even dared to peer down over its edge. The fog was clearer below now and I thought I could make out some trees or green bushes.

Holmes confirmed that he too could see them, adding, 'I believe we are no more than perhaps two or three hundred feet from the top of that foliage.'

This news gave me fresh confidence and I worked with a will to descend those last few hundred feet. Of course there were thoughts of how unfortunate it would be to fail on the last lap of what had been an horrendous descent and a terrifying experience! There were indeed trees to aid the last part of our downward climb. I gratefully transferred myself to a palm, the descent of which seemed like child's play compared to what we had been doing on the cliff face. I fastened my belt around the bole of the tree and held onto it like grim death, working myself down those final thirty or forty feet. Holmes did the same and we collapsed at the base of the palms, forgetting our hunger and thirst in our relief at being on firm ground again.

I must tell the reader that I have never been very fond of coconut, but those that we discovered at the base of the trees were quickly opened by hurling them at rocks, providing us with both solid and liquid refreshment.

As we wandered into the clearing which lay beyond the trees I was struck by the eerie beauty of the place we had come upon. As I gazed upward the sun still shone, though waning, through the rainbow fog, looking for all the world as if it were streaming through huge stained-glass windows into a vast cathedral. The desert had ended with that huge line of cliffs and here there were grass and plantains, punctuated here and there with pools of clear water. The end of the world had indeed given way to the beginning of Eden!

We had collected our scattered wits and with them our few remaining accessories. We had these in our back packs and our rifles hung once more from our shoulders as we made for a pool where we thought to drink and freshen ourselves. I have faced many dangers alongside my friend and colleague Sherlock Holmes, but never before or since anything like as terrifying as that climb down to this promised land. May my future life be long or short I do not think I will be able to erase that terror from my mind.

But to return to the story which I relate, we did in fact both drink and bathe at one of the many pools and later, much refreshed, we strode confidently in that same compass direction that we had followed now for weeks in our search for Marrafaze. We could perceive no sign of habitation or life, other than some distant ostrich and onager. We thought at one point we had spotted a group of men but it turned out to be a small troop of baboons, of that maned, silver Arabian variety. We gave them a wide berth and, remembering my experiences with baboons in the past, I was comforted that we still had our rifles.

Then as the sun was fast disappearing we spotted some Bedouin on camels. Friend or foe, there was no chance to hide or flee for they had clearly seen us and were making in our direction. Their leader rode swiftly to us, and causing his camel to kneel he leapt from its saddle and confronted us. He was a large man with a vast black beard and the robes and headpiece of a Bedouin. I noticed that his camel harness was richly decorated with silver bells and ornamentation and his musket, which he carried almost carelessly, was studded with what appeared to be precious stones. He spoke in a form of Arabic which we did not understand. We tried to speak to him in French with which we had been able to communicate with Bedouin before, but this time there was a blank response. More or less as an afterthought, I imagine, Holmes addressed him in English.

'We bring greetings from the great queen, Victoria!'

It was clear that he did not understand what was said, but equally clear that he had heard English spoken before, because this time there was no blank stare and it was clear that English speech had some effect upon the others, still mounted upon their camels, as well. They looked at each other and muttered one word, a name familiar to us, that of 'Abdul'.

Holmes said to me, 'We have found the fabled Marrafaze, Watson, but let us take care not to mention the name they have just uttered until we can be sure that it will not produce unfortunate results. We are merely diplomats as far as they are to know.'

I took the point of his advice and spoke to the Arab spokesman. 'From Britain . . . to see your Sheik!'

The fellow surveyed me with severity and I noticed with interest that there were red henna streaks in his black beard. He signalled for us to hand him our rifles, which somewhat reluctantly we did. Fortunately my revolver was in a pocket of my tunic rather than in its holster. A camel was brought forward and made to kneel that we might both clamber into its large saddle. Then the beast got to its feet and the Arab shouted, 'Imshi, hut, hut, hut!' and we were on our way to we knew not where.

'My dear Westlake, I believe we should again start to get used to our *nommes de guerre*: with luck we are at last upon our way to see the Sheik of Marrafaze. It has been an incredible journey and you will dine out upon it for years should we ever return to London!'

'Holbrook, do you think our return is in doubt?'

'I certainly do, unless there is some kind of short cut of which we are ignorant. Mark you, we might be able to start off with some more practical mountain-climbing equipment!'

We soon could see a distant habitation which I estimated we would reach within some thirty minutes or so. I could make out palm trees and buildings of some kind, but more, I could faintly see what looked like a kind of minarette. As we drew nearer I estimated that we were approaching a settlement that was perhaps the size of a very small town or large village by our own standards. First we came upon tents with simple Arab people peering out of them and later these gave way to typical desert huts and finally we were before an eastern palace, rather like a miniature version of that pavilion raised by George IV at Brighton in Sussex.

'Upon my word, Westlake, if we had not experienced that nightmare expedition I would think that we were dreaming of some Shangri La of sheer legend. The tops of those minarettes are of pure gold as far as I can see with the naked eye. This must be the residence of the Sheik, and it is my profound hope that he speaks a known European language; one known to us, that is!'

I responded, 'If not there may be some sort of aide or chancellor who could act as an interpreter?'

We were taken through a paved entrance toward a large apartment which we entered to find an imposing Arab, beyond doubt the Sheik, seated upon a huge chair which raised him up in an impressive manner. He was surrounded by servants who came and went upon various errands and missions, but another figure stood beside him and this was a very different sort of person to all of the others. He was darker of complexion and whilst robed he wore no headpiece, displaying a wild head of black unruly hair. His facial expression was also rather wild and he was the only clean-shaven man that we had encountered since our arrival.

Holmes remarked to me, very quietly, 'This will be the Grand Wazir mentioned by Abdul. I must say he does not inspire me with confidence regarding our future!'

We stood at the foot of the short flight of steps which were before the throne. The Sheik rose to his feet in astonishment at our appearance. Instinctively we both bowed our heads and he addressed us in the local Arabic, obviously asking questions. Holmes answered in English, taking the diplomatic envelope from his back pack.

'Great Sheik of Marrafaze, we are delegates from Great Britain and servants of Her Majesty Queen Victoria. We bring Her Majesty's greetings.'

The Sheik, rather to our surprise, replied in an English of sorts. 'I understand, Efendim; I speak a little English. I sent my eldest son Abdul to your country, to one of your great seats of learning. When he returned he imparted at least some of your language to me, though he later proved unworthy and I was forced to disown him. He left here some time ago, and I have no idea to where he went. But at least he did one good thing in teaching me the English. Forgive the way I speak it, for since he left I have no one to converse with save in our native tongue. It is papers that you hold?'

Holmes handed the papers to the Sheik who seemed to have some difficulty in reading them, despite the use of a huge and ornate pair of spectacles which he produced. But I felt that he had grasped the main burden of the document.

'So Holbrook Efendi and Professor Westlake, I will have a bungalow, I think you would call it, prepared for you and you may join me for dinner tonight when I will try to entertain you. One moment, my Wazir wishes to consult me . . .'

The wild tribesman conversed with the Sheik and I felt that what he was saying about us boded ill. After a quite lengthy conversation the Sheik turned to us again with perhaps a shade less warmth in his manner.

'I have given my Wazir some idea of our conversation and of what is written in this document. He has reminded me that I must consult with him and others before I make comment upon your mission. No doubt when I entertain you at dinner I will be in a better position to talk further. Please withdraw and be rested: I have noticed that you have had a hazardous journey and I will supply all of those things which you might need.'

I followed Holmes's lead in making a salaam as we backed respectfully away from the throne.

The apartment to which we were taken was indeed a splendid one, light, airy and spacious. We made first use of a kind of sunken bath, and later dried ourselves and changed into the splendid robes with which we were supplied. Then we sank gratefully upon the pile of cushions upon the floor and once the serving people had departed we discussed what had happened. We were no doubt safe in speaking in English before them, but took no chances.

I opened the conversation. 'What did you make of it all, Holmes? Oh, do not scowl so, for we are quite alone! The Wazir looked as if he might frighten Attila the Hun!'

'Yes, Watson. And of course we already knew that he would be a thorn in our flesh, being in league with Abdul's brother, Mustapha, whom we have yet to meet. I observe your whimsical remark concerning Attila the Hun with due amusement, but would remind you that there may well be an even more terrifying Hun involved in this matter!'

His remark of course reminded me of our conversation with Mycroft concerning the real purpose of our visit: to investigate some deadly mineral in which the great Empire of Austro-Hungary was unduly interested. More to the immediate point I brought up the matter of the Sheik's health.

'Did you notice how unsteadily the old man rose from his chair? His eyes rolled frequently and his hands shook. I imagine he is suffering from a condition of the heart which may be as serious as Abdul thought.'

'Watson, Abdul is not a medical man, but you are, yet I feel that you have both been deceived regarding his condition. I have observed very similar symptoms among the opium smokers of Limehouse.'

'Surely opium poppies are not native to these parts?'

'No, but there well may be similar narcotic plants that are. I have had considerable experience of such things, and I know the symptoms well.'

'So he may not be quite as unwell as Abdul feared. "Near to death" I believe was the expression he used?'

'He may have been nearer to the truth than you think, my dear fellow. He is probably being supplied with the narcotic by the Wazir, who also shows signs of some such influence. But remember, that which takes away pain and brings pleasure can kill, should the dosage be suddenly increased.'

Later we were collected and escorted back toward the palace and whilst on the way there a quite interesting incident occurred. We came upon a crowd of Arab youths playing a game with a bat and some kind of ball.

Holmes looked on with interest, saying *sotto voce*, 'So unless the crusaders played cricket we are looking upon a recently introduced game, possibly brought back by Abdul from the university.'

I replied with equal softness of tone, for despite our

escort having no English we were taking no chances whenever the name 'Abdul' came into our conversation.

'You think it is cricket that they are playing?'

'Yes, or rather a variation of it which is suited to the terrain and available materials. You will notice that some rocks have been arranged to form a wicket and some sort of a cricket bat has been fashioned from a metal, obviously by a swordsmith.'

I noted the strange triangular blade being wielded by one of the boys and said, 'I don't think "W.G." would approve of that bat, and I wonder what that is that they are using as a ball?'

As if in answer a small rounded stone flew toward us to be neatly fielded by Sherlock Holmes. He was about to throw it back to the bowler when the members of our escort scared off the youngsters by shouting at them in irritation. As the boys ran off Holmes shrugged and dropped the stone into a fold of his robe. Meanwhile our chief escort tried to explain something to us in Arabic, but all we could make out was the name 'Abdul' and the distaste with which he pronounced the name. So Holmes had been right in supposing that cricket was one of the unpopular innovations that Abdul had brought back from England to Marrafaze.

Holmes chuckled, 'Poor lads, they probably worked long and hard on that piece of rock to make it such a near perfect sphere. If I get the chance I will return it to them later.'

I said, 'Our escort reminded me of one of those keepers in Regent's Park, spoiling the pleasure of urchins playing upon the greensward!'

Meanwhile we had re-entered the palace for the promised meal and entertainment. The latter a performance by nautch dancers, whilst the former appeared to be some kind of goat meat stew. As honoured guests certain unspeakable portions of the goat were offered to us, the Sheik watching closely to see that we consumed them, the Wazir evidently encouraging this. Holmes whispered to me, 'Take that goat's eye that is being offered to you and swallow it down, there is a good fellow. Remember, you are doing it for Queen and country!'

I took his advice and swallowed the eye, pretending to chew it with relish. This seemed to produce a calming effect upon the Sheik, but the Wazir looked at me with eyes like daggers. Then when this main course had been cleared away we were given sweetmeats which were pleasant enough to drive thoughts of the goat's eye from my mind. But evidently the Sheik believed in mixing business with pleasure. The company present formed a circle, just as they had when watching the nautch dancers; but this time it was for serious business.

The Sheik gave us some intimation of the form that this would take. 'Efendim, I will now hold what you might call a court of justice. I am holding it now so that you may study our methods and realise what a very civilised and advanced country you are in.'

What happened next was an interlude that amazed me and filled me with disbelief as to what I witnessed. A series of prisoners were brought in, one after the other, each in chains, their misdeeds being evidently read aloud and the Sheik dispensing what was intended to be justice. There was no evidence presented, no witnesses called, but the

Wazir held a willow wand before them and if it twitched they were found guilty and dragged screaming away; if it did not they were released from their chains and respectfully backed out of the palace.

After a series of these episodes I exchanged glances with Holmes, then whispered, 'Upon my word, he is nothing short of being a witchdoctor, he himself alone deciding the guilt or innocence.'

Holmes was similarly astounded. 'Who would have thought that such a ceremony could take place in this year of nineteen hundred. This Wazir has more control over the Sheik than I had dreamed. I feel that we should intervene but doubt the wisdom of such a step.'

Then came the incident which decided Holmes to do just that; moreover the opportunity presented itself. A litter bearing the dead body of a man was brought in, followed by two women, evidently his wives. They were quite plainly distraught and terrified. The litter was placed down before the Sheik who beckoned to us to join him.

His words were disturbing to say the very least. 'Holbrook Efendi. You have had an example of our very efficient system of justice. As a wise man of your Queen I would like you to pass judgement upon this next case. You see before you a man who has defaulted in the matter of paying his taxes. The Wazir had told me, when he was suspected of hiding his money, that he had put a spell upon the man which would kill him within seven days if he were guilty. Bear in mind that he was in excellent health and young in years and this has been the fifth day since the casting of the spell. Had he been innocent he would still be alive. Now, by our laws, the two women, his wives, must be put to death when the guilty verdict is made. However, I will leave the matter to you. But bear in mind I will expect some manifestation if you bring in any other verdict than a guilty one!'

Holmes beckoned me to follow him, which I did, and he led me to where the body lay. Very quietly he said, 'Make as quick and thorough examination as you can that we might gain some idea as to the cause of his death.'

The Sheik and the Wazir showed some surprise and even consternation as I made as thorough a check as I could, given Holmes's added suggestion that I do it quickly. I could find no injury of any kind, but certain signs suggested the possibility of poisoning and I conveyed this thought to Holmes. He nodded and drew my attention to that which my examination had missed; the sole of the departed man's left foot.

'Why, there is a thorn embedded in it.'

'Yes, an acacia thorn, harmless enough on its own. But I suggest that you remove and examine the thorn.'

I did as he bade me and found to my surprise that the thorn had been treated at its sharp point with a purple liquid. I could only agree that the fellow had been killed through poison introduced into his foot by this means. Holmes quietly deduced, 'I can only think that our friend the Wazir planted the thorn, perhaps near an entrance to the man's house which he knew that he alone was likely to use when barefooted. It was possibly planted in the ground with its point upward. The man's sudden death without seeming cause bore out his prophecy. We must find a way to save the lives of these two women who are clearly innocent.'

We tried to explain the cause of death to the Sheik,

who, I thought, seemed to find wisdom in our words. But we left out the account of the Wazir's evil behaviour for reasons of practical diplomacy. Holmes pleaded for the lives of the two women but after the Sheik had consulted with his Wazir he said, 'I can only do as you request if you can bring some sign that the gods would want this. If you are as powerful as my Wazir you will be able to demonstrate your affinity with one of the powerful gods. Can you perform some miracle that is beyond the powers of the Wazir?'

Although he had seemed an intelligent, if misguided, man, the Sheik did none the less appear to be developing a mockery in his manner. Then this became even more manifest after he had turned to the Wazir and evidently informed him of what he had said to Holmes. My friend retreated a step or two and whispered to me, 'Upon my word, we are like characters dreamed up by H. Rider Haggard. What would Allan Quatermain have done?'

I tried to remember my youthful reading of *King Solomon's Mines*, then said, 'He would have turned an eclipse of the sun to his advantage, or got his friend to take out his glass eye.'

Holmes laughed bitterly and said, 'I know of no natural phenomena that might come to our aid, and we have not a glass eye between us. If only I could dream up some chicanery to rival the feats of our wild-eyed friend.'

The Sheik's eyes were upon us and I sensed that he was about to signal an execution. But I have never ceased to marvel at how such emergencies can so quicken and clarify my friend's wits.

He brightened and said, 'I have it!'

He turned his back upon us all for a moment, moving his head and shoulders as if in some kind of communication with godly beings. Then he turned and walked toward the throne, saying, 'Most powerful Sheik, I have been in consultation with one of my most powerful gods; for I have many: he has suggested that he should make a sign that you would recognise as being of unearthly origin.'

The Sheik's interest was aroused. 'What form will it take, Holbrook?'

Holmes's reply was as great a source of amazement to me as it was to the Sheik. He said, 'The great god of necromancy has suggested that if he were to stop my pulse it would surely convince you of my power, through him, and the wisdom of my suggestion regarding justice in the case of the dead man's wives.'

The Sheik laughed aloud and translated Holmes's words to the Wazir who laughed even more hugely. Eventually they both quietened and the Sheik spoke again, 'Forgive my merriment, Holbrook, but for you to claim to collude in causing something to happen which is even beyond the powers of the great and wonderful Wazir makes me laugh. However, as a representative of the great Queen I must show you respect, however wild your claim. If you were to be able to cause your pulse to stop, shall we say for a man to walk twice completely around this building, I will do as you suggest in the case of these women.'

Holmes agreed to these terms and the Wazir was allowed to nominate a man to perform the encircling walk. We noticed that he chose the most elderly man present and seemed to be giving him instructions which I guessed took the form that he should take his time. Holmes extended his left arm and offered the wrist to be held. The Sheik himself placed his fingers around them, saying, 'O Holbrook, I feel a very strong pulse indeed from the veins of your wrist. Tell me when you are ready for me to dispatch he who will twice walk around the building?'

Holmes swayed and trembled, which I took to be an exhibition of mumbo-jumbo. Then he said, 'I am ready!'

The Sheik threw up his left hand and the old man left the building. The monarch's right-hand fingers did not leave their encirclement of Holmes's left wrist. He said, 'Your pulse is still steady . . .'

Yet within a few seconds his expression changed to one of surprise. He looked at the Wazir and spoke in Arabic. The wild man replied angrily and the Sheik said to Holmes, 'Your pulse does indeed appear to have stopped, but the Wazir thinks that this is just a momentary pause which cannot long continue.'

After what seemed like an age a watcher near the entrance signalled, I guessed to the effect that the old man had made one circuit of the palace. The Sheik's wonder grew, and so did the anger on the face of the Wazir. Holmes, a superb actor, a sad loss to the London stage as I have often remarked, shook and rocked to and fro as if in league with the supernatural.

At long last, the 'runner', having delayed his return as long as he possibly could, re-entered the apartment at a snail's pace. The Sheik stood with his fingers still searching Holmes's wrist in disbelief. The Wazir also tried to find a pulse but could not, clearly. He could hardly deny this manifestation in the view of evidence presented to his monarch.

'Holbrook, you may consult with this god and persuade him to once again allow the blood to course through your veins.'

There was some more superb acting from Holmes, and eventually I could tell that the Sheik could again feel a pulse throbbing. He dropped Holmes's wrist and backed into his throne.

I had no idea how my friend had managed to perform this seemingly impossible manifestation. To my medical knowledge only the skilled use of a tourniquet could have produced such an effect but this could scarcely have been achieved by one man, standing alone. Of course I could not tax Holmes for an explanation until the evening was over. The two women had been set free, and Holmes had 'judged' several other 'cases' before we left for our beds, and all but the most obvious and blatant wrongdoers had likewise been released.

I made sure that we were not observed or heard before I mentioned the matter of the pulse-stopping phenomenon. Then I said, 'Upon my word, Holmes, in Suffolk, a couple of hundred years ago you would have been burned at the stake, or at the very least tested in a ducking stool!'

But Holmes made light of the matter. 'It was elementary, my dear Watson. Some years ago I was able to assist the Yogi Carib Dumbah when he gave an exhibition in London. You may remember that he thrust hat pins through his lips and the flesh of his arms and evidently could read messages written upon a blackboard when his eyes had been covered with dough and then bound with many yards of bandage. He also walked upon hot coals and picked up pins with his eyelids . . .'

I was impatient. 'Holmes, what has that to do with your stopping your pulse?'

'Hear me out, Watson, have patience. I was able to restore to him some valuable property thought to be lost. In his gratitude he showed me how to perform various seemingly impossible feats, the stopping of the pulse among them.'

I had the most horrible feeling that he was going to leave the matter to rest, but he relented.

'You see, Watson, the effect is gained by holding a small, hard rubber ball in one's armpit. If the right pressure is maintained it will cause the pulse to stop beating.'

As a medical man I, of course, understood the principle, but was still puzzled.

'Will you kindly tell me where a hard rubber ball mysteriously appeared from, to conveniently lodge itself in your armpit?'

'Sarcasm does not become you, Watson. Do you not remember the boys' game of cricket that we witnessed and the small stone sphere with which it was played?'

I understood. 'Of course! You fielded it when it was thrown, and as I remember you slipped it into your robe.'

'Correct, and far from it conveniently finding its way to my armpit, I assisted its passage when I went into a sort of trance prior to stopping my pulse!'

'I see. Simple when you explain it.'

'It was indeed, Watson, the skill was in my making use of the coincidence of having that ball in my robe and remembering the Yogi. I was taxing my mind with what he might have done in the same tight spot as I found myself.'

Suddenly I felt ashamed at having dismissed Holmes's

remarkable display of quick thinking and retention of knowledge as 'simple'. He had a remarkable mind, I knew; a repository for all manner of facts and knowledge which he could seemingly file for reference and use at the right moment.

CHAPTER SEVEN

The Tomb of Terror

The following day presented us with a series of surprises, the first being in the change of the Sheik's manner toward us. We were taken to him and found that two lesser thrones had been placed beside his own, one on each side of it. In these we were invited to sit and I was a little apprehensive when I saw the Wazir, somewhat in the background and in a seemingly evil mood.

The Sheik made quite a speech for our benefit. 'I cannot read the English of your documents, Efendim, but I recognise the seal of Her Majesty. I have decided to make you my closest advisers after the events of last evening. My Wazir will, of course, be still a valued ally, but I realise that his power is not as great as yours. In return for your advice and confidence I must, of course, do what I can concerning these matters which the papers mention. Please tell me what it is you seek in the land for Marrafaze?'

I was all for plunging in at the deep end and bringing up the subject of the unfortunate disowned Abdul, but I sensed that this could be too early a point to do so, with the Prince,

Mustapha, seated before us on the steps. I decided to take my lead from Sherlock Holmes, who made no mention of Abdul, but said, 'Our Queen is interested in some strange mineral with which she could prevent some foreign devils from upsetting the peace of the world. I know little of the form it takes, but I know that if it is not carefully controlled it could destroy us all. Wicked men might come here and even kill to possess it.'

The Sheik nodded and said, 'I know not what it is you refer to, but some foreign devils came here and found something to interest them near the graves of the infidel crusaders of so long ago. When we remonstrated with them for disturbing the dead, they threatened us with muskets that fired without reloading and without use of powder or ramrod.'

I asked, 'Could you describe these foreign devils?'

He pulled at his beard and his eyes narrowed as he said, 'They were dressed in clothing like that in which you arrived but very much less worn. They had strange helmets, a little like those of the infidel crusaders. I could not converse with them because they spoke in a strange tongue; a little like yours, yet I could not understand it. They too had papers, but the crest was not that of your esteemed Queen, rather it had a great bird depicted, like an eagle!'

Holmes took a precious vesta from his robe and struck it, allowing it to burn for a while before blowing it out. Then with it he sketched the emblem of the Austro-Hungarian Empire on the back of our letters of introduction.

The Sheik recognised it at once. 'Yes, that was the style on the papers; the big bird and a crown, I remember.'

Holmes asked, 'What became of these men?'

'We put them both to death that they would trouble us no more. I had their muskets for a time, but I destroyed them by fire, thinking it safer to do so. We burned their other things too and have prayed much that others like them would not come here.'

I thought that Holmes was taking a great risk when he asked, 'May Professor Westlake examine the spot near the crusaders' graves where this substance was found which caused such trouble?'

'Of course. I would like your opinion on what it was there that attracted them. Through the years there have been other men who took oddments from the place, and then departed in peace. Do you think they showed the pieces to the evil ones and caused them to come here at such cost of effort? I do not need to tell you how hard it is for those from the outside world to penetrate our peaceful land.'

I mentally said 'amen' to that. Holmes added, 'I think it likely that the legends about Marrafaze and some kind of important mineral got back to an extremely wicked man, the Kaiser.'

'He is a king?'

'Yes, of a land called Prussia, but he rules far beyond its borders, and even parts of the world quite close to here.'

Then the Sheik changed the subject, asking us all manner of questions about the land of the Great Queen and her colleagues.

'Does she have a Wazir?'

'Why yes. She has had many during her long reign. Gladstone and Disraeli being perhaps the most celebrated.'

'Did they advise her well?'

Holmes and I exchanged glances, then he said, 'Sometimes, certainly they saw our nation prosper and expand.'

I felt that we were on dangerous ground considering our present problems in the African continent. I asked, 'Do you think I could examine the ground near the graves of the crusaders?'

Mustapha and the Wazir were in the party with the Sheik which accompanied us upon gloriously caparisoned camels to a place in a desert about ten miles from the main town of Marrafaze. On the way we passed a few encamped Bedouin who all threw themselves down before their ruler who benevolently bestowed largesse upon them.

Eventually we reached a small collection of graves which had stones to mark them, obviously older than would be seen in even the longest established English cemetery. Of course the word 'crusaders' at once brings to mind those sarcophagi carved with depictions of armoured knights with hounds at their feet. But these markers were far more primitive and were engraved with a barely discernible series of inscriptions in what I took to be a simple, early Arabic form of language. There were stylised illustrations, rather like those found in the tombs of the pharoahs. Near to these graves was an area which had obviously been disturbed, though not in recent times. I called for a shovel and one was produced, with which I dug, very gently. Holmes stood watching, his eagle eyes scanning every turn of the sandy soil.

I turned up various artefacts, most of them scarcely recognisable. There was that which might have once been a leather drawstring pouch, and a metal gauntlet, or part of one. A few stones and small pieces of rock were turned up, Holmes depositing all of these in his back pack. The Sheik watched with interest, but the Wazir, although curious of our actions, seemed extremely uninterested in the articles that we collected.

Mustapha asked a question, through his father, which was translated as, 'Why on earth should you, and the foreign devils, be interested in those useless pieces of stone?'

I tried to explain the point of archaeology, through the Sheik, but he remained unimpressed. The Wazir was fast losing interest. To be truthful, I was singularly unimpressed with what I had turned up myself, and said as much to Holmes when we were again alone.

'All that glistens is not gold, Watson, but by the same token all that is dull and dirty is not useless. Minerals take many forms: for example, Turkish silver is not as valuable as the more refined variety. But I think we can be reasonably sure, though we have no means to prove it, that we are dealing with gold here. Undoubtedly the Germans were as passingly interested in the crusaders as are we ourselves. This is what interested them, though I am sure that the Kaiser is ignorant still of the existence of gold here or that they found it.'

'You mean that none of the so-called archaeologists survived to reveal their findings?'

'For certain, Watson for another, larger party would have arrived by now. Mycroft will indeed be most intrigued with our discovery.'

'But Holmes, I thought he was interested in the possibility of a mineral that would revolutionise warfare?'

'Gold is such a mineral. War is expensive, and there may be as much gold to be mined here as there is in South Africa, enough to capitalise the largest land and sea forces that the world has seen. Mycroft may have suspected that it was gold that the Germans were after.'

'Would he not have told us just that?'

'Probably not. My brother is an excellent fellow in so many ways, yet devious. He knows enough about me to realise that a search for mere wealth would not have captured my imagination. He intrigued me by the possibility of saving our great empire from an attack with some secret weapon. I came here for two reasons, that being one of them, the other being the possibility of restoring our client to his rightful inheritance, an aspect which we have as yet neglected for reasons of survival. But we must start to give it thought.'

'I have noticed, Holmes, that there is a rapport between Mustapha and the Wazir.'

'It has not escaped my notice and I am somewhat concerned for the safety of the Sheik. He is too convinced of the loyalty of both of them for me to make an accusation, but we must observe and be alert at all times.'

I put away the articles and rocks which we had unearthed in my back pack after Holmes had inspected them all carefully. He had lost his lens, but used my reading spectacles, which I had fortunately carefully preserved in place of it.

The day that followed found us again digging near the graves of the crusaders. As before we were not left alone, but fortunately the Wazir, very intrigued by our activities, had seemingly no idea that the pieces of rock and stone could be of any possible value. It was not very long before the place where we were digging seemed to be worked out. I said, softly, 'Obviously it is surface gold and does not go deep. This means that we must find another likely spot to dig.'

Holmes shrugged and his whole manner toward the enterprise appeared to have changed. He addressed me quite loudly. 'Come, Professor Westlake, we have done enough for now. Let us seek an audience with the Sheik that we may pay him our respects.'

We were taken to the throne room where the Sheik greeted us and asked if I had discovered anything of interest. 'Professor, have you found something that is good to eat or smoke? I do not understand what you seek.'

Holmes glared me into complete silence and said, 'Great Sheik, we have been unsuccessful in finding other than a few pieces of rock and some extremely old artefacts. Come, let us talk of other matters that are of more interest.'

The Sheik clapped his hands and a hookah was brought, the smoking of which he invited us to share with himself. I had noticed that he was extremely shaky, and that his eyes glistened as the hookah arrived. I did not doubt that it was well charged with the opiate of which he was partaking so frequently. He handed the mouthpiece first to Holmes who took a mouthful of smoke. His expression did not change yet he caught my eye and I sensed that he was warning me concerning the strength of the opiate. It was my turn and I took a small puff which made my head spin, despite the fact that I did not take any of it into my lungs. But the Sheik took huge puffs which seemed to have a strong effect upon him.

At length he spoke, in a rather erratic manner. 'Honoured Efendim, you have been with us for only a short time yet have already endeared yourselves to me, and to my

Wazir who does not usually take kindly to those he does not know well. He it is who has suggested that I make you both my principal advisers. This means that I will consult you both at all times. I have agreed and I am sure you will do the same.'

The Wazir grinned at us evilly, as did Mustapha, and it was clear that we could not safely refuse this suggestion.

The Sheik continued. 'You will aid me in judging at my courts of justice as you so recently did. Your mysterious powers will help me to be sure that no injustice is ever done! You will be able to advise me on so many things and I know that your great Queen would be delighted to let me keep you here. You will not only be my confidantes for the rest of my earthly life, but when I cross into the great sleep you will remain at my side and continue to give me your friendship and wisdom.'

His eyes rolled in a bizarre manner and he swayed in a manner that made us anxious. That night we dined with him and ate quite heartily, but declined the hookah, though not daring to criticise his own indulgence. Then, when he was clearly too weary to talk to us further, he caused a litter to be fetched and was taken to his repose.

Then, when we had retired to our apartment, I noticed that there was a strange atmosphere, by which I mean concerning the manner of those who served us. They retired somewhat hastily and were replaced by armed warriors who stood in the doorway as if on guard, and when we glanced at the window spaces we could see that these were guarded also from the outside. We decided to test this rather worrying change of policy by attempting to casually stroll out through the doorway like two English gentlemen wishing to indulge in a constitutional. However, it was not to be, with the guards barring our way, though with nothing threatening in their manner. We were none the less uneasy and made no attempt to make any sort of exit through the windows. I asked Holmes what he made of this sudden worrying development.

He said, 'Watson, I realised that it was pointless to refuse the Sheik's offer to be made permanent members of his court, preferring to bide my time and choose the right moment for us to do it. My greatest unrest was when he mentioned that we would be his advisers even after his death. You will be familiar with the ancient Egyptian custom of entombing the king's servants and advisers with him, so they could serve and advise him even in the next world? If anything happens to the Sheik, and he has left any kind of instructions to the effect, we may well never be seen in London again, save perhaps a century or two from now, as exhibits in the British Museum.'

Grim humour indeed from my friend, but a glimmer of hope occurred to me. 'Well, Holmes, for one thing the Sheik is not yet dead, although I'll grant you that he is heading in that direction, and the Wazir would doubtless himself be on such a list of advisers should the Sheik die. You are also assuming that Marrafaze has such a tradition anyway!'

Holmes nodded thoughtfully. 'You could well be right in all these points that you make, my dear Watson, and I sincerely hope that this is so. But the death of the Sheik is imminent, through the direct actions of the Wazir who encourages his use of powerful narcotics. But he would scarcely do this if he knew that it would lead to his own demise. I have no doubt that if such a tradition does exist here the Wazir has found a way to preserve his own life. He has probably convinced the Sheik that his own advice to Mustapha is vital. But the Sheik appears to have taken a liking to ourselves and might enjoy our company in the next world.'

His words made me shiver, but I tried to be optimistic. 'Let us hope we are able to make some kind of escape before the Sheik expires, or before you frighten me to death! Come, Holmes, you are beginning to sound as if you believe in the next world after all.'

'Oh, I discount nothing, Watson, but I would rather prove my own theories in that direction at a much more advanced age! As for making our escape, I believe that such could only be gained by subterfuge. At least I have tobacco, for this is a three-pipe problem!'

Holmes charged his pipe and lit it from the oil lamp which stood upon the table; conserving no doubt the few vestas that were left to him.

He settled upon an ottoman for a period of quiet contemplation, but hastily rose again after taking just a single puff of the pipe. 'Upon my word! Watson, would you be so kind as to take a puff at my pipe?'

I did as he asked, and reeled at the strength of the opiate that had contaminated his tobacco. It was my turn to exclaim, 'What does this mean, Holmes?'

'It means that my tobacco was adulterated whilst we conferred with the Sheik. The intention is possibly to reduce my mental powers and save the Wazir from any possibility of an attempted escape. Try your own tobacco, Watson.'

I did as he suggested but found it just as I would have

expected it to be. Holmes hastily substituted some of my shag for the mixture that had contaminated the bowl of his briar. He said, 'I imagine the Wazir thinks that he can create a craving for this opiate in me, little realising that my system is used to regular doses of my seven per cent solution of cocaine. For the first time in your life, Watson, you should be glad for my background in that direction. Fortunately you had kept your own pouch within your robe.'

I slept but fitfully as Holmes consumed vast quantities of my tobacco. I dreamed a dreadful nightmare in which the Sheik had died and Holmes and I were interred with him; yet we were not dead as were the other slaves and advisers. In my nightmare we were entombed alive and were dying of slow starvation, whilst surrounded by untold wealth and embalmed corpses. I awoke to find Holmes still reclining, but wide awake and giving every impression of having remained so throughout the night. He was dreadfully cheerful, and I dared not relate my nightmare for I needed his hearty support.

'Watson, I have thought long and hard and have come to the conclusion that short of escaping from this place entirely, our main hope is to familiarise ourselves with the traditions which surround the passing of a Sheik in Marrafaze. We can convey the idea that such research is part of the learned study that you are here to carry out. At the same time we must be alert and watchful for any lifeline that man or fate might extend to us. Be of good cheer, dear friend, fear nothing, for it is fear that is the greatest detriment to clear thought. Let us assume that the worst might happen and plan what we will do to combat it. Now it occurs to me that if we were to request of the Sheik that we might be allowed to explore much further afield . . . to seek minerals and artefacts. Whilst he might insist on our being accompanied I have little doubt that he will give his permission. We can also imply that we are disappointed to be held under house arrest.'

His words gave me renewed hope. After all, who better to have as a colleague than Sherlock Holmes when faced with this alarming situation; already his sharp mind was exploring every avenue and might well find others even more encouraging.

Then suddenly our thoughts and conversations were rudely interrupted by the arrival of a party, led by the Wazir and Prince Mustapha. They entered, having been bowed deeply in through the doorway, and stood there with a triumphant air about them both. They spoke in turns and then they spoke at once, and when we failed to understand they raised their voices as if we were deaf rather than non-Arabic speakers. We caught the odd word such as 'Sheik' and 'imshei'. I could only translate that we were wanted urgently by the ruler and felt that a chance to talk with him was just what we presently needed. But I noticed a certain unease that had crept into Sherlock Holmes's expression; an unease which only a very close friend might recognise. As we were escorted from the apartment, sure enough he said, 'I don't like the open triumph and arrogance of their manner, and I warn you, old friend, to be prepared for the worst.'

Where he had filled me with confidence, he now warned me to expect the worst. Yet I mused that this was something better than receiving some great totally unexpected shock. That the Sheik had died before we had a chance to consult him? Surely not! But this was the 'worst' and so it was what I steeled myself to find. In this I was not wrong, for inside the entrance to the palace there was a great deal of weeping and moaning and the waving about of deeply draped portraits of the Sheik. But in the throne room our worst fears were established as having been justified. There was a great open-topped sarcophagus in which lay the Sheik, surrounded by deeply bowed mourners of both sexes. Most of them we had never seen before but we considered that they must be wives, nephews, nieces and confidantes. Most significant of all, they were in chains! But worse was to come, for shackles were quickly placed upon our own wrists and ankles with a suddenness and rapidity that was indeed unnerving. Worse, there was nothing we could do, no one that we could turn to because the Sheik had been our only English-speaking lifeline. If anyone else in Marrafaze might understand a word that we said they had never given any indication of the fact.

Yet Sherlock Holmes stood erect and spoke with confidence and considerable volume, 'If anyone present can understand English, French or any other European language, will they please make themselves known to me? I am a servant of her gracious Majesty Queen Victoria whose dominion extends from Great Britain to all known continents. If we do not return, an expeditionary force will undoubtedly be sent to search for us! Now please, if you understand me, kindly arrange for myself and my colleague to be released. We also mourn the passing of your Sheik who had become our friend, but we cannot be treated in this fashion.'

It was an impressive speech, but it produced no encouraging response, just blank stares, shrugs and even the odd sly grin. We had no reason to be optimistic now, especially when we were marched away along with all the other prisoners and placed in a large apartment with barred window spaces and doors.

Holmes turned to me as we settled into the straw which was the only furniture in the place, and said, 'Well, Watson, at least we can dispense with the niceties of false identity now. We can address each other openly by name.'

'A poor return for being cast into this dungeon, which, however large, is the only way to describe it, along with all these other unfortunates. We are no better off than they!'

Holmes considered before he replied. 'We are in a slightly better position than they, my dear Watson. You see, they are entirely resigned to their fate. We at least will fight like tigers to regain our freedom should the chance present itself. I suppose it is too much to hope that you still have your service revolver?'

'I have it, Holmes, but it is in my back pack, which is in our original apartment.'

Holmes breathed hard and deep before he replied, 'We must try and regain that satchel, Watson, though I have no great faith in our being able to do so.'

Holmes made a commotion, so much so that a guard came to threaten him to silence. However, Holmes treated him to a demonstration of pantomime to rival anything ever done by the *Comédie Française* or any other theatre group. He pointed to a string bag which one of the other prisoners had. Then he pointed to me and made me turn that he could point to my back. Then he asked me, 'Have you anything about your person, Watson, which we might offer him as a bribe?'

I had very little in my robe save my reading spectacles. I could not think that these could be very much use but Holmes pounced upon them eagerly. He put them onto his nose and inspected the palm of his own hand. He conveyed surprise at what he saw, then placed them upon the nose of the Arab. That worthy was at first bewildered by all this but then he imitated Holmes and inspected his own palm. Then he started, inspecting in turn other things around him, soon realising that an object had to be held within a few feet for the glasses to have any effect. But eventually he indicated by actions that he would like to own the glasses and I mused that his sight might be similar to my own; in which case he would indeed be holding a prize! Holmes nodded but took the glasses from him, and repeated the pointing to the bag and my back. Understanding dawned in the Arab's face. He nodded and departed, I hoped to fetch the bag.

I had some doubts that he would bring it to me but Holmes was more optimistic. 'Watson, despite our situation and imprisonment these are not evil people. The man is honest, otherwise he would simply have confiscated your glasses; it is we who are devious!'

I had to admit to this possibility and Holmes was proved right when the Arab shortly reappeared with my back pack. He gave me this and then made circles with his two index fingers and thumbs, holding them to his eyes. I grinned and nodded, handing him my spectacles. He was delighted.

Holmes turned to me and said, 'Do not on any account open the bag or inspect the contents until a better opportunity arises.'

Wise words, which I heeded.

It was in fact only when darkness had fallen that I was tempted to peer into the bag to be sure that it still contained those things that I had known once to have been there. To my joy it was so and the revolver was there, with a few rounds of ammunition and the other things that we had dug up near the crusaders' graves. I informed Holmes in a whisper.

He equally quietly replied, 'Watson, just leave it as it is. The sleeping guard may waken at any moment and we do not wish to have it searched. The idea of a weapon being concealed in such a small bag would not have occurred to the Arab who returned it to you, in this land of muskets and huge knives.'

Then we discussed the matter of how long our incarceration in our present apartment might last. Holmes thought that it would not be for long.

'Most North African peoples have a very quick way with the disposal of the dead. I imagine that climate has promoted that tradition and the tradition is strong even where the embalmed bodies of monarchs are concerned. With the dawn will probably come the day of the entombment of the Sheik. Let us hope that it will not be our own farewell to this life, or worse.'

'What, Holmes, could be worse for us than being put to death?'

'Watson, dear friend, I will not answer, and it is my sincere hope that you never learn it.'

Sure enough with the coming of dawn we were marched out of our prison and made to follow the sarcophagus which was being pulled upon a series of rollers by a team of camels, all gloriously caparisoned with cloths and ornaments.

There were soldiers and others, all in similarly decorative attire, some bearing likenesses of the Sheik and gorgeous banners and pennants. There was much wailing and moaning again, and some people ran about as if near insane with grief. We just kept our heads down but remained extremely alert. The procession took a long time to reach its goal which was well away from the centre of the habitation. Indeed, when we finally came to a stop it was at what seemed like the entrance to a large cave in the side of a sandstone hillock. The sarcophagus was borne into this place by a great many hands, and as we were forced to follow we saw that there was an opening in the ground, suggesting access to some kind of cellar. This proved to be so and as the coffin was lowered we followed by means of rude stairs that had been hewn in the sandstone.

The apartment into which we descended was well lit by hanging oil lights and was filled with objects which I would under happier circumstances have described as attractive. There were silver bowls, engraved by craftsmen, carpets of finest embroidery, statuettes of questionable artistry, and coffers that could for all we knew be full of treasures. Some of the bowls contained fruit and sweetmeats which Holmes whispered to me were for the refreshment of the Sheik whilst on his journey to the next world. There were also hookahs and a quantity of the doubtful tobacco that had undoubtedly been the cause of his death, and flasks which doubtless contained liquid refreshment for the monarch.

A ceremony was carried out in which the Wazir took a leading part, and then to our horror a series of executions were carried out. The prisoners were lined up, with the exception of ourselves, and made to kneel. A huge Arab with a scimitar-shaped weapon stood at the far end of the line from us. He stood behind the first prisoner and to our horror (I dream about it still) he beheaded the poor fellow. I have seen some bloodcurdling sights in my time but have never before or since witnessed execution of a ritualistic style. The fact that he went right along the line of prisoners and despatched each of them in turn was made even more bizarre and horrific by the fact that none of the victims showed any sort of reaction. I believe I knew for the first time the fullest meaning of the expression 'like lambs to the slaughter'.

In a quavering voice I asked Holmes if this was not the right moment to use my revolver? But he inferred that it would be a pointless demonstration of futility.

He whispered, 'You have no chance to save them, Watson, for see how many muskets are trained just in case of some sort of reaction. It would be best to save your bullets for ourselves, when we know what our fate is to be.'

I did not like the sound of these words; did he mean that I might need to shoot my friend and then myself? I hoped that there was something else in his mind. I was soon to find out, because the persons concerned with the ceremony began to back out of the tomb. (For this was the only way to describe the place where we found ourselves.)

Holmes whispered, 'Watson, our chance may be about to present itself. We must wait until the last of them have backed out and then make a rush when it is least expected. Shoot if you must, but I fear that may be futile; being fleet of foot might allow us to gain that thickest of thorn scrub which I noticed as we came in. From there we could better defend ourselves with your weapon. If we were able to hold our position there until dark perhaps we might stand a remote chance of making our escape.'

I had no great hope that he could be right, but I knew that this was no time to be faint-hearted. 'I'm right beside you, Holmes, ready for anything.'

His rejoinder quite touched my heart. 'It was ever thus, dear old friend.'

But alas, our plan was thwarted, for we had misjudged the speed with which they would seal the tomb entrance. At the very second that the last Arab had backed out through the entrance some huge boulders began to block it. Then there were more and more and we were prisoners in what I can only describe as a tomb of terror.

CHAPTER EIGHT

A Living Death

Despite the closeness of the atmosphere I was gripped by a ghastly chill. I have often heard the expression, 'my blood ran cold'. What else but icy fear can course through one's veins when you are entombed with an embalmed monarch and eight or nine of his now dead relatives and retainers? The fact that the place was filled with treasure with which one could become extremely rich indeed in any other place did not help our situation at all. The reader will probably be asking himself, 'Why did they not try to push the boulders once the soldiers were likely to have departed?' Dear reader, despite our both knowing how futile this would be we tried indeed. After a quarter of an hour we sank exhausted. I believe I was the first to speak.

'I should have ignored your advice and used the revolver earlier to force our way out!'

'You would be already dead, as would I had you tried it.'

'We are as good as dead now. We are buried alive, to starve or die from lack of air.'

'Not quite. I do not believe that the Sheik has any use

now for the refreshments for his journey that they have left him. Neither has any one of these other poor souls. We will survive for a week, maybe longer. There is air in here, though where it comes from I know not. If it were airtight the lamps would have gone out.'

I was determined to be a pessimist. 'These dead bodies will poison what air there is and we will be without light when all the oil is burned.'

'We will ourselves extinguish all but one lamp. I have a few vestas with which to relight one of them when the first is exhausted.'

He was as determined to be optimistic as I was to be such a dismal fellow. He went on. 'Eventually they may return to inspect the tomb. If we can survive we may get another chance of escape.'

We extinguished all but one lamp. He was right, we would have light for many days at least. We sampled the fruit and sweetmeats deciding that there were enough comestibles to keep us alive for many weeks if severely rationed. Liquid was more important and there were bottles of wine which might keep us alive, though I would have traded them all for one bottle of clean water. We searched for other comestibles or objects that might aid our survival in some way, but found little else to encourage us. Then Holmes got an inspiration based upon one of his deductions which was little short of being quite brilliant as far as our furtherance of existence was concerned. He would not explain why he wished me to collaborate with him in a certain manner at first; although later I realised that he had not wished to cruelly raise false hope. But I will cease to be mysterious and explain exactly what occurred. When we had been in the tomb for some thirty-six hours (I was fortunate in still having been able to retain my hunter) my friend bade me to unhook the single hanging lamp and bring it to one of the wooden arks, which we knew from a cursory inspection contained only precious stones and trinkets.

His next words filled me with thoughts that our ghastly experience was beginning to play tricks with his mind. 'Watson, give me your revolver. I am as you know a fair shot: hold the lamp high with your left hand.'

I did as he bade me and observed that he checked the revolver to ensure that it was loaded.

Then he gave me fresh instructions. 'Pick up one of the swords which are beside the body of the Sheik, and when I give you the word to do so, throw open the lid of the ark and stir its contents vigorously with the sword, then stand well back, leaving the lid raised.'

I could not imagine why he instructed me thus, but followed those instructions to the letter, throwing back the lid upon his exclamation 'Now!' and stirring the gems within. Then, as I stood back, holding the lamp aloft I almost dropped it in amazement at what I saw and heard. For from amid the stones there emerged a serpent-like shape, which raised a hooded head and hissed horribly. There was a sharp crack, as Holmes fired my service revolver and the creature dropped, inert save for the odd twitch, among the glittering debris. I gasped, 'Good heavens, what is it?'

I still could not grasp what had occurred, for it was as if some supernatural guardian of the treasure had arisen, only to be destroyed by Holmes's remarkable single shot.

Holmes, however, brought logic where fantasy had been in my mind. 'It is a cobra, Watson, of the most deadly variety. I am ashamed to have put you in by far the worst of the danger in that I could not warn you lest you should falter in your actions. Moreover, I could not have changed places with you because I knew that it was I who stood the best chance of killing the creature with one shot. Had I missed it might have escaped and lurked in the shadows as a sinister menace to our future rather than an aid to our salvation.'

I was still bewildered. 'How on earth did you know it was there?'

'I was not certain, but I suspected that it might be. During a doze an hour or so ago I suddenly recalled that the Egyptians of old used to place an asp or a cobra in each treasure box to deter tomb robbers. One learns these things, Watson, only half believing, but just once in a while they prove true and of use.'

'Holmes, I admire the train of thought which has produced this dead reptile, but what possible use has resulted from the nightmare experience you have put me through, I should be delighted to hear!'

Perhaps I spoke too warmly, through reaction to the shock I had received.

But Holmes answered calmly, almost kindly. 'My dear fellow, as a seasoned campaigner have you never roasted a snake?'

'Never. The thought revolts me.'

'When you have sampled it, Watson, you may change your mind and will then rejoice in the fact that each of these arks probably contains a similar guardian.'

I was unconvinced. 'How, pray, shall we roast it?'

'Over the oil lamp, upon a sword point.'

It took another twelve hours, with just my small ration of fruit and sweetmeats — plus a glass of wine — before I was ready for Holmes's culinary experiment. He cleaned the snake with a knife, rather as one would gut a fish, and then roasted a portion of it just as he had suggested that we should do. I have to admit that the result was quite tasty, or was to me at that time. (Though I have no desire to add cobra to my regular diet.) Certainly I could see that if each of the boxes contained a reptile our lives might be extended by a week or two beyond our calculations. We tried to rely upon the juice of the fruits to quench our thirsts, for the wine tended to defeat its own object by making us still more thirsty, however much we should drink.

Day and night were the same in the tomb, but I marked the passing of each twenty-four-hour period upon the wall with a knife point. We tried to sleep at regular intervals upon the heaped animal skins and lengths of cloth for which the Sheik was deemed to have use in the next world. But in truth we were wakeful for most of the time. We passed the seemingly endless hours in discussion of adventures old and new and, ever optimistic, of adventures purely imaginary which might be yet to come.

The worst, however, was starting to manifest itself after we had been entombed for about seven days. The bodies of the slaves and others were beginning to decompose and the stench started to be very unpleasant. We moved our living area further and further from them for there was no way we could effect any sort of burial. We so wished that they had been embalmed like the Sheik.

Then one night (for night I calculated it to be) something occurred which was to lead eventually to our salvation.

I was dozing, and awoke to find Holmes sitting bolt upright, his hawk-like nose pointing, as if attracted by some occurrence. He saw that I was awake and placed a long slim finger to his lips. Why, I could not imagine, for to my knowledge we were alone in this grisly place. I followed the direction of his gaze, imitating his alert silence.

Then I saw what his sharp eyes had spotted in the dim light of a single oil lamp. A sandy-coloured shape was streaking around among the bodies of the slaves.

I breathed, 'It's a jackal!'

It was indeed one such carrion-eating desert dog and before long our silence and stillness were rewarded with the sight of the disgusting little canine feasting upon human remains. At first my thought was to scare it away, but I realised that Sherlock Holmes would already have done that had there not been a good reason for his inaction. Eventually the little yellow dog retreated to the back of the tomb, dragging a human arm with him.

After the creature had disappeared from our sight into the unlit area of the tomb, Holmes arose and took the lamp, and whispered, 'Let us see where our canine friend has gone to, Watson.'

By that flickering light we searched every inch and every cave-like crevice of the apartment, but could find no hidden lair or answer to the enigma of the appearing and disappearing scavenger. Eventually we gave up our stealth and discussed this bizarre turn of events.

'Watson, at worst that disgusting creature will rid us of the problem of the decomposing flesh. At best he will help us to find a way out of our predicament.'

'But Holmes, we have searched, and there is no way in for the animal.'

'We have not found it, but it exists, otherwise the jackal appeared from nowhere, by magic! Come, it could not have hidden in here without being eventually discovered. We have to remember that like our own native fox he is lithe, slim and canny. I'll wager a jackal could gain entrance and exit through a seemingly impossibly small gap.'

'But Holmes, we have searched everywhere by the light of our lamp and found no such gap.'

'Granted, but it is there. The jackal is nocturnal, therefore it is dark outside. If we were to search as thoroughly by day as we have by night we might see some tiny glimmer of daylight.'

My impatience grew as we waited for that time when I calculated the midday sun might be at its brightest. Then when that time arrived we again made our tour with the lamp without success. But Sherlock Holmes was ever inspired and enterprising.

He said, 'Watson, do you think you could endure a period of complete darkness? I have a few vestas left for relighting the lamp and I believe we might more easily see some shaft of daylight that way.'

He held up the lamp that we might have one last look at our surroundings but hesitated to extinguish it. He seemed to be studying its vapours. Then he said, 'We may have a short cut to our investigation, Watson, for notice how the small plume of smoke from the lamp seems attracted by one of these fissures. I will put out the lamp, if you will first place your hand upon my shoulder.'

In that manner I was able to follow his movements in the dark and as he led me into the recess that had attracted the smoke I saw to my joy a small shaft of light. As we drew nearer to it we could see that it was indeed a very small gap in the sandstone, with daylight undoubtedly upon the far side of it. Perhaps four or five inches deep it was no more than a foot wide and it was hard to believe how even the very small jackal that we had seen could have squeezed through it, but when Holmes relit the lamp we perceived that there were sandy hairs encircling the gap and it became clear that this had been the creature's way in and out.

'I remember once, Watson, hearing of a mouse imprisoned in a kettle managing to escape through the spout! Now let us see what the possibility is concerning the enlargement of this slot.'

We worked upon the thickness of the sandstone around the gap for many hours with a sword and a small axe which we discovered among the artefacts which had been thought useful to the Sheik in the next world. It certainly proved useful to Holmes and me in this world! By the time night began to fall we had enlarged the space so that a jackal would be able to pass through it with no difficulty whatsoever. Then, exhausted, we took some fruit and a little wine and slept until dawn. If the jackal revisited us we did not hear it as we slept the sleep of the fatigued.

Because we were working upon sandstone it made our plans possible, but by no means easy. In fact it took three full days before we had reached the point where any kind of escape seemed even vaguely possible. But our spirits were high, for we now at least had a little daylight and the air was getting more fresh by the hour. We were now in no great hurry to finish the excavation, for our survival seemed ensured and our only real worry for the future was in the manner of the place in which we would eventually emerge. We tried to calculate exactly where it might be.

Holmes drew a diagram upon the loose sand that we had deposited upon the ground through our excavation. 'You will see, Watson, that I believe we will emerge into that desert area which is immediately behind the palace.'

'Surely we would do well to steer clear of that area, Holmes?'

'That depends upon our future intentions. If our desire is to leave Marrafaze without attaining our goals I suppose we could try and make our escape, stealing away in the night perhaps? But just how we can leave this place I am not sure. Remember we are in a vast extinct volcano. We risked life and limb in lowering ourselves into this place. It would be even more difficult to climb back up again. I believe our wisest course is to brazen it out and make a triumphant return to the palace in the form of supernatural beings who cannot be killed. We might even still achieve our goals and leave this place in some degree of comfort. Perhaps you would care to put forward an alternative plan?'

I thought long and hard before saying, uneasily, 'Well, we would hide out in the desert and live off the land . . .'

Holmes was dismissive. 'For ever and a day, Watson, oh, come my dear fellow! Better to continue to stay in the tomb than take up an all but solitary nomad existence. No, Watson, we must be bold or all is lost.'

He was right, of course. I had no real desire to be one of only two pale-skinned Bedouin, without even a camel between us! At least a bold course of action held out some kind of chance to return to England, home and Baker Street.

But there remained another day of excavation before we needed to come to a definite decision. In fact it was, I believe, at the end of our fifth day of chipping and banging that the hole was large enough for us to emerge without undue difficulty. We both climbed in and out a few times before settling back in the tomb for the night. Then at dawn we collected together that which we felt might be of use, though there was little enough that would be of help to us in the outside world. Being on the outside of the tomb was a joy for a while, but the novelty soon wore off as we tried to discover our exact situation. We found a pool and satisfied our thirsts with long deep draughts of the first clean water to which we had gained access for a long time. This gave us strength, and we demolished a few wild dates and felt our strength reviving.

Eventually we discovered that Holmes's diagram had been fairly accurate and we came quite easily upon the rear portion of the palace. It seemed to be unguarded, which was not as surprising as one might at first think. After all, there were no rival tribes involved, and Mustapha, aided by the Wazir, appeared to have dealt with rivals nearer to home. There might well be no one in Marrafaze beside ourselves who might dare to question the evil duo's authority.

As we had agreed between ourselves we walked into the first entrance that we could find without any kind of stealth. We were, of course, still in the robes in which we had been entombed. We were somewhat grubby, but none the less held a certain dignity. We encountered a few servants who did not seem to realise the enormity of the situation of our reappearance. However, eventually one, more astute than the others, recognised us and betrayed our presence. By this time we were resigned and prepared for this.

As the Arabs gathered and raised a riot we walked, unhindered by any sort of physical contact, into the throne room where sat Mustapha, with his infamous Wazir seated beside him. He gazed at us with a glassy stare and shouted and pointed in our direction. The Wazir seemed even more amazed, and far more concerned. His manner changed to one of apprehension as he conversed with Mustapha who eventually addressed us, seemingly having forgotten our lack of Arabic. Holmes and I responded in English, shouting loudly and threateningly. I prayed that this tactic would work, and that we would not be hacked to pieces by the guards. But I was relieved to find that we seemed not to be in any danger. Far from it in fact, for we were offered gilded chairs in which to sit and delicacies to eat and drink.

I asked Holmes, 'Do you think that this means that our plan has worked?'

'For the moment, Watson, but they will eventually discover our means of egress from the tomb. Until then I imagine we are safe enough and must work upon our new personas as being reborn in some unaccountable way.'

I was willing to think that Mustapha might well believe us to be the spirits of our earthly being, but, and Holmes agreed, the Wazir was far less gullible and likely to feel that we had somehow managed to escape from the imprisonment that he had arranged for us. No doubt he now wished that he had resisted the temptation to exert such extreme cruelty in not having us executed along with the other victims. We could only hope that the possibility of escape through the rear of the tomb might not occur to him and that he would spend quite a lot of time trying to find some other answer to the enigma. Meanwhile he could go so far but no further in his relationship to Mustapha, who obviously believed that we were ghostly beings and must in that case hold certain fears concerning his own part in our incarceration.

We were given an apartment, more splendid than the one we had occupied during our previous stay at the palace. We could hardly enjoy its affluence lest its comfort and ease should prove to be a very temporary arrangement. However, we did manage to relax in sleep. Indeed we were both so drained of energy through the events of the past ten days or so that we both almost literally collapsed onto the padded couches that had been provided for us.

After a dreamless sleep of some seven hours I awoke to find Holmes seated upon a pile of cushions, cross-legged like a tailor and smoking his pipe.

His morning greeting was one of complaint. 'Watson, I would give one of those gold nuggets from your back pack for an ounce or two of the Scottish mixture! This which passes as tobacco in Marrafaze is strong and black but has not mellowed. I fear that most of them rely upon the opiate that they mix with it to make it palatable. I trust you slept well? I allowed myself four hours of slumber, but thought it wise to get my mental and physical powers working well lest this day should present problems for us.'

I realised that I had allowed myself to fall into a rather lethargic state; the reaction to our ordeal. Now, he had reminded me, I must be alert and ready for anything.

I asked him, 'Do you have any advice, based upon your contemplations?'

'No, Watson, simply to keep your mind and body alert and ready for anything. We are not as stoutly shod as I would wish, but you still have your service revolver. Whilst I pray that you will not need to use it, be of good heart; you could dispatch half a dozen of their musketeers in the time it would take to reload their museum pieces.'

About five minutes later a party of attendants arrived, bowing and indicating that we should follow them. I tried to study their attitude toward us but it was difficult to define. They were hardly bowing and scraping to us as they had been upon the previous evening, yet they showed no aggression.

I remarked upon this to Holmes who replied, 'Be vigilant, Watson, but show no fear or suspicion of them.'

This was easier to say than to carry out, but I walked as upright as I could manage and Holmes remained calm to any casual observer. By the time we reached the throne room I had in fact almost convinced myself that my detection of a change in their manner might be just in my imagination, but the Wazir's look of evil triumph could not be mistaken. Mustapha made us a long speech which I assumed to be more for the benefit of his colleagues than for ourselves; for he well knew that we had no Arabic to speak of. I tried to read something from the manner in which he delivered his speech. I seemed to detect an air of 'How could you deceive me and think to get away with it' in his style. He was cheered on by his evil little Wazir who shouted some sort of encouragement every time the monarch paused for breath.

When the speech was finished we were bundled out of the palace, with Mustapha and the Wazir following with their servants. When they were mounted upon camels I assumed correctly that we were to be taken a fair distance. We were escorted to the tomb entrance by which time a large number of the populace were to be seen in the background. Mustapha made what appeared to me to be a similar speech to that which he had made at the palace. This time, however, I noted with a certain amount of interest that the crowd were a little half-hearted in their applause.

Holmes had noticed this too. 'Watson, I feel that the people of Marrafaze are not entirely happy that Mustapha has inherited the Sheikdom. This seems to me to be our only hope for salvation. The Wazir is out for our blood. I have no doubt he has found our means of escape, but whether he will reveal this depends upon whether he is representing us as men or devils. The latter might be his best chance of rousing the people to his cause.'

A vast number of labourers were sent for and with levers and much effort they managed to open the tomb entrance. My heart sank as a lamp was lit and we were marched back into our previous place of incarceration. This time, apart from the soldiers who controlled us, the Wazir and his Sheik, were what I can only assume to be a representative group of the population of Marrafaze. A rather dour, silent group who nodded in obedient assent whenever they were addressed. The lamps revealed a gruesome sight, for since our departure and doubtless aided by the enlarging of the rear aperture it was obvious that many jackals had visited to feast upon the bodies. The Wazir seemed to be making a big point of this and it crossed my mind that he was accusing us of being cannibals.

Holmes agreed with my thought and enlarged upon it. 'I think the Wazir is saying that we feasted on the bodies to give ourselves the strength to use evil powers to mysteriously escape from this dreadful place. I believe our only hope is to illustrate to these observers our real means of eluding a long, slow death.'

I understood exactly what he meant and tried to visualise what would happen if we made a dash for our escape hole. But the way to the rear of the tomb was barred by our captors.

Holmes indicated that we might stand a better chance by doing the unexpected. 'Watson, we must make a run for it from the front of the tomb and around to the rear. They will pursue us, but if we are lively in movement we may escape being shot by their clumsy muskets. If and when we arrive outside the exit hole it is to be hoped that the delegation from the people will still be with them and will understand that we are mere mortals!'

The reader will hardly need to be told that in the face of great odds against it our plan worked. (Otherwise, obviously, you would not be reading this account!) We made a desperate dash out of the tomb and by erratic movements as we ran, and through the element of surprise, we reached the place from which we had escaped without even a minor wound between us. Moreover it was to our advantage that the delegation of citizens arrived before the royal party. We pointed and showed by actions how we had accomplished our escape, even showing them the sword and the axe. By the time the Wazir had arrived there was a great deal of enlightened muttering going on. The Wazir recovered his composure, if such his behaviour could ever be called, and was soon making some kind of impassioned speech. But he had lost the fine edge of his control of the situation and Mustapha was looking very doubtful about what had occurred. We were still most certainly under restraint by the soldiers, but there was less conviction in the way even they behaved toward us.

'We are not out of the woods yet, Watson.'

I realised how true were Holmes's words. The position however, was not one of falling out of the frying pan and into the fire. We stood in the square in front of the palace, surrounded by what seemed to me to represent a fair proportion of the population of Marrafaze. Mustapha's throne had been brought from the palace and he was seated upon it. The crowd that surrounded at a fairly respectful distance appeared to be one of a more surly nature than that representative few who we had encountered. I knew not if their surliness was directed toward their ruler or ourselves.

What next occurred perhaps transpired to be the greatest surprise of my not uneventful life. I have oft experienced coincidence and events which seemed to have some kind of divine intervention. Holmes might deny the latter but could not question coincidence even when there was a logical background to it.

CHAPTER NINE

Mycroft to the Rescue!

As we stood there in that sandy square before the palace our future was very much in the balance. It appeared to us that we were being tried, as men or devils or both! The Wazir had pranced in front of us for a considerable time, performing various 'miracles' which evidently were the basis of his case against us. He lit a small fire and threw some kind of red powder into it which made quite a spectacle. Then he held a conch shell before us in turn, which resulted in a trickle of blood-red liquid pouring forth from it.

Holmes muttered to the effect that it was controlled through a hydrostatic principle. 'As a man of science you will doubtless have recognised that he removes his thumb from a small hole in the shell before the liquid emerges. A cross between a flute and a pipette!'

How he could make learned jokes at such a moment I did not know, but I was cheered slightly by the seemingly growing doubt upon the face of Mustapha. Then, when the executioners were beckoned by the Wazir, Mustapha rose and waved them away. After that he appeared to be having some sort of major disagreement with his adviser. Then silence reigned and there seemed to be a major battle of wills between the monarch and he who appeared to be midway between a witch doctor and a prime minister. What might have happened next who can say, but what did was this . . .

Quite suddenly, through the rainbow mists and cloud there appeared a vast sphere. At the sight of it the crowd were as amazed as I, and perhaps even more apprehensive. As for Sherlock Holmes, he was as calm as ever as he surveyed this 'apparition', and saying, 'Bless my soul, Watson, I had hoped for some diversion to occur but I never thought it would arrive in the shape of a balloon!'

Of course in the year of 1900 captive balloons with their passenger baskets beneath had long emerged from the Jules Verne stage with the general public. For half a century serious experiment had produced such apparatus of more and more sophistication. Evidently the balloonist no longer relied upon the wind or needed to risk the life and limb of those upon earth by the discarding of heavy sandbags; it was all done by valves and syphons. In any case we were assured that the new spirit-driven flying machine which was like a winged motor car would shortly make the balloon a museum piece. Events of the twenty years that followed would prove this to be so, but at that actual moment in time the balloon was the only means of air transportation that would carry its passengers for more than a dozen miles. It could travel far, if not fast, and had become relatively safe. This particular balloon was huge, it was colourful, and I considered it heaven-sent. Its valves hissed as one of the passengers in its basket threw down an anchor, and several persons descended by a rope ladder. They guided it down and secured it and I saw that within its basket there were still two persons; the balloonist, and beside him a vast man in immaculate aviator's dress, complete with helmet and goggles. This huge man was the last to descend and did so only when the others had provided every possible means for his safety in so doing.

The Arabs were silent now, including Mustapha and the Wazir. I turned to Holmes and asked, 'What do you make of it?'

He all but snapped, 'Our salvation!'

'Yes, but who do you suppose the big fellow is, the smart one with the silver helmet and huge goggles?'

'Oh, I know who he is. I'm more interested in identifying one or two of the others.'

I was infuriated. 'Holmes, please enlighten me concerning the big man!'

'Does he not seem a familiar figure? He is my brother.'

'What?'

'Certainly; it is Mycroft, and I was never so glad to see anyone in my life.'

Holmes infuriated and reassured me at the same time. The two principal aviators moved toward us and the crowd drew back in apprehension. The taller, broader man removed his helmet and goggles to reveal that he was indeed Mycroft Holmes. He extended a hand to us in turn.

'Sherlock, Watson, how splendid to see you both. You see I waited for a decent length of time before I tried to find out what had happened to you. I managed to get the government to mount a proper expedition with champagne and a crowd of askari. We followed your trail but lost it at the edge of a sort of volcano rim. Fortunately I had a balloonist following us in case he was needed, and by Jove he was! How on earth did you two get down here? We found nothing but a few tent pegs just over the edge of the bluff. Don't bother to answer, you can give me the details when we are back at the Diogenes, which I intend to be very soon. Do you know I travelled through the desert on an elephant? The only way to travel, brother mine. Faster than a camel; the only drawback is that you need a lot of mules to pull the water tank; elephants drink a lot of water you know, but they are an extremely comfortable mode of transportation. Well, did you find what I sent you here for?'

Sherlock Holmes was almost as outraged as I was at Mycroft's cavalier treatment of us. 'Upon my word, Mycroft, you can be a pompous ass at times. First I have to make some sort of peace with Mustapha who sits upon the throne. You could have been a mere diversion rather than a permanent salvation.'

'Oh I doubt that, Sherlock. You see I have brought the rightful Sheik, now that the old one has died.'

I interrupted, 'How could you know that?'

It was Sherlock who answered, 'He can see that the old Sheik does not sit upon what is obviously the throne. He has brought Abdul, who has no doubt told him a great deal about the possible situation here.'

Abdul stepped forward and removed his helmet. The crowd roared with approval. Abdul told us, 'They are shouting that the gods have sent back the rightful Sheik in the shape of my humble self. My wretched brother is thereby disgraced. See how he skulks away . . .'

But there was nothing joyful or triumphant about Abdul's manner, for in our preoccupations we had perhaps forgotten that he had lost his father. Estranged they may have been, but it must still have been a great shock.

Holmes commiserated with him briefly, then said, 'I cannot tell you how glad I am that at last we have a translator. Your father spoke good English and was a great help in that direction. He was a fine man, which is more than I can say for the Wazir! Your brother I judge to be more misguided than sinful.'

That night there was a splendid banquet in the palace, with Abdul in his rightful place upon the throne. The Wazir was banished and Mustapha hovered around his brother seeming to want to atone for his sins. We told our story, although Mycroft anticipated our words in a thoroughly irritating manner. When we told him of the chests of precious stones he said, 'Perceive you opened them with great care. The cobra's sting is invariably fatal.'

I knew better than to ask him how he knew about the cobra, or indeed how he seemed one jump ahead of our story. After all he was Mycroft, with possibly a more brilliant brain than his brother. He knew that we had made some sort of discovery from the way I clutched the bag that had served as my back pack.

He demanded to know, 'You have discovered the minerals? What form do you think they take?'

We told him that we had only discovered gold and showed him the pieces from my bag. He examined them carefully, squinting through a gold-rimmed monocle. 'Gold of a most remarkable quality. This is better news than that of a wonder mineral that would make explosives. If we make a treaty with Abdul here, which I feel sure we can, we will be able to buy all of the explosives in the world . . . well . . . almost!'

We took Mycroft to the place where we had found the gold, near to the graves of the crusaders. When it was explained that we had found no more, the mineral expert that Mycroft had brought with him said, 'No matter, where there is a surface deposit like that the area is bound to be flush with the lovely stuff. It often happens in extinct volcanoes, but not usually of such superb quality. I tell you, gentlemen, when we open up mines here we will surpass anything that comes from Kimberley, and with none of the troubles with the Boers!'

Sherlock was unusually thoughtful, eventually saying, 'I want Abdul and the people of Marrafaze to benefit greatly from this. I would want to see substantial assistance with the provision of schools and hospital facilities as well as financial provision. Please let me cast an eye over any treaty you may draft before he signs it. He is after all my client.'

Mycroft later laid the treaty, written in his own stylish hand, before us.

Sherlock scanned it swiftly and nodded in approval. 'I notice, Mycroft, that the first and third sheets are the original document, the one you intended to get Abdul to sign before my suggestions. I am glad you decided to be generous after all.'

Mycroft smiled enigmatically and replied, 'Of course, despite the same ink and my usual paper being used you recognised the difference between ink that had dried in a temperate zone and that which had more swiftly dried in a tropic clime.'

'Yes, brother mine, and you had changed the nib.'

'To an exactly similar Waverley, but of course you noticed the very slight distortion of writing produced toward the end of the document through a minimal crossing of the points of the nib, suggesting that I would have to have changed it.'

'The paper of the middle sheet had a minor difference too, although from the same original packet . . .'

'Which you knew because it had been cut in exactly the same position through the watermark . . .'

'Yes, but it was fresh from your writing case; the other sheets had been stored in an outer pocket of your portmanteau . . .'

'The slight scent of cigars upon sheets one and three?'

'Exactly, and you well know the answer to the question that has come into your mind. We do not become partners in my endeavour because you are far too lethargic, and have things of both national and international importance to concern you. I am amazed though that you managed to shift yourself from that armchair at the Diogenes and make such a journey, and in a balloon! Quite out of character, my dear Mycroft.'

'My dear Sherlock, does it not occur to you that my concern for the safety of my younger brother might have something to do with it?'

'Not for one second. Your sole interest was in the possibility that I might have found the mineral that you mentioned. I imagine your dismay to find only gold.'

'Oh come, Sherlock, gold, as I have already indicated,

will buy any amount of weapons of destruction. Beside which there may be no war, and gold is extremely useful in times of peace as well.'

'But you and I both know that there will be a war, within perhaps ten or twelve years, more terrible than any conflict in history and one in which most of the nations of the world will be involved.'

'Sherlock, although I have no intention of joining you in your enterprise there is no reason why you should not join me in mine.'

'Oh come, you well know half a dozen reasons . . .'

'You mean aside from your complete lack of interest in political matters, that you have no affiliation with any church, and that you bow to no one save the Queen herself?'

I found this dialogue between the two greatest brains in the British Empire or possibly even in the world, fascinating, as ever.

Of course Abdul signed the treaty when Sherlock Holmes advised him to do so. Then, when Mycroft and his colleagues had departed for their beds, Holmes gave him some advice as we shared a goodnight hookah.

'My dear Abdul, accept everything that is of use that is offered to you and use it to further the advance of your people and to strengthen your own position. But please remember that these advantages may not be of a lasting nature: put everything you can into reserve, and develop your natural advantages. Above all, try to keep your little Sheikdom out of a very great conflict between two great powers which will have consequences in this continent eventually, and not just in that where it begins.'

On the following day we were taken in the balloon to Tangier, where we rested and purchased some European clothing. (Mycroft demanded this, saying, 'At present I cannot take you anywhere!') Then, within a week of travel luxurious in comparison to that which we had recently experienced, we found ourselves safely back at 221B Baker Street. It had been a great adventure and one that we would never forget, but 'east, west, home is best', and Mrs Hudson's steak and kidney pudding compares favourably with any exotic fare that we had encountered. Moreover, I can always be sure that there are no surprises, such as optical organs to be discovered amid the suet and gravy. It was over such a delicious meal that Holmes and I discussed our adventures and of course as ever his last declarations on the subject had a 'sting in the tail'.

I asked, 'I have been meaning to enquire of you, Holmes, just why you gave that particular form of advice to Abdul?'

He sighed with contentment as he disposed of a beautiful amalgum of suet pudding, steak, kidney and mashed potato before he replied. 'Watson, I believe I gave the new Sheik, our client, some excellent advice. After all, the prospectors, assayists and miners will not be in Marrafaze for ever. In fact they might be there for a very short time indeed. But if he is astute, and I believe he is — and he has a university education to back up his wits — he will conserve the vast amounts of aid which will be extended to him.'

'How long then do you think it will be before our government withdraw their support and interest?'

'A year and a half or perhaps two years, no longer.'

I admit that I started at his words. 'You think that the gold will be exhausted in such a short time?'

He was playing me like a trout I would later realise as he said, 'Gold, what gold . . . you mean you really believe that they will find gold in Marrafaze?'

'But of course I do, for did we not ourselves turn up a small fortune in gold nuggets in about an hour?'

'After which we found no more.'

'True, but you heard what Mycroft and his colleagues said, to the effect that there would be surface gold throughout the area.'

'I very much doubt it. You see the gold which we found was taken to Marrafaze by the crusaders who had doubtless found it somewhere else upon their long journeys. I am no assayist, but I know a little about precious metals and I recognised that those nuggets had not been excavated from that sandy soil. There were traces of the terrain from which they had originally yielded to the greed of those adventurers who claimed to be fighting the Lord's battle. We found artefacts that had clearly belonged to the so-called crusaders at about the same depth as the nuggets. These included a hide pouch in which the nuggets were probably conveyed to Marrafaze. I observed from its style that the pouch had not been made in Africa but bore all the signs of having been fashioned in Europe in the twelfth century.'

To say that I was stunned would be to understate the case. I could see that his bombshell placed an entirely different light upon the treaty between Her Majesty's government and the Sheik of Marrafaze. But Holmes was very casual about the whole thing. When I accused him of deceiving his own brother he was warm in his own defence.

'Oh come, Watson, you know that Mycroft is as canny as I to say the very least, and indeed I consider that he passes me by in that particular. The government will scarcely miss what they spend in Marrafaze and the treaty could be useful should the Kaiser ever send his minions in that quarter again.'

I was still astonished at his guile. 'What will you say to Mycroft in a year's time when no gold has been found?'

'I will tell him the truth, just as I have told it to you, Watson, and he will laugh, if I know my own brother.'

'But suppose he does not see the humour in the situation?'

My friend's eyes were twinkling as he played out his reply, obviously enjoying my reactions to it. 'Why then, Watson, then I will give him the mineral that he sent us there to find.'

'The mineral?'

I confess that during our death-defying adventures in Marrafaze the mineral had quite disappeared from my mind until Mycroft had so unexpectedly appeared, and been so dazzled with thoughts of the gold that he had seemed to lose interest in all else.

'Yes, Watson, that mineral which by legend might change the whole character of modern warfare. Surely you did not think that I ceased to search for it, especially as I had realised the truth about the origin of the gold from the very start.'

'You mean . . . you found it?'

'I certainly found something that could well prove interesting to the bloodthirsty heads of government.'

'But where, and what form does it take?'

Holmes put down his knife and fork and took a vesta box from the pocket of his elderly faded pink dressing robe. (He had upon that first night home reduced his usually high standards at the dinner table.) He rose and beckoned me to follow him. I protested that I had not yet had my rhubarb tart which I knew to be in the offing. Holmes snapped at me, 'You have the rest of the evening, the rest of your life, to stuff yourself with puddings, Watson. Just follow me to my bench if you require an answer to your questions.'

I followed him as he went to his bench and cleared his test tubes and chemicals, pushing them aside to make a space. Then he opened the vesta box by pushing out its tray, and poured a few grains of a sandy-looking substance onto the wooden bench top. He carefully closed the box and returned it to his pocket.

Then he pointed toward the hearth and requested, 'Be so kind as to pass me the coal hammer, Watson.'

I did as he bade me and he took the implement firmly in his right hand. Then, after a few admonishing feints with the hammer he brought it down sharply upon the little sandy pile. Nothing happened and he returned to the dinner table. I followed him back there, somewhat bewildered. Was this some sort of experiment that had failed? I said nothing and by the time Mrs Hudson had removed the remains of the pie and served the pudding I had tried to put the matter out of my head. Why ruin a good pudding of rhubarb tart and custard with thoughts of a pathetic little pile of sand?

Then it happened, after I had demolished half of my favourite dessert there was a minor explosion from the chemistry bench!

'Good heavens, what was that?'

I'll wager I more than merely started, whilst Holmes still attended to his pudding. However, eventually he put down his fork and sauntered over to the bench where again I joined him. I gazed in amazement at the little pile of what looked like now blackened sand.

Holmes threw back his head and laughed out loud, a rare manifestation with his character. 'Oh Watson, I am sorry if you were startled by my little experiment, but I could not resist illustrating for you its full effect! You see when we were excavating our way out of that dreadful tomb I noticed once or twice a certain number of very minor explosions which seemed to occur with no particular cause. You were so intent upon saving our lives that I don't think you even noticed them.'

I said, 'Not surprising. I was very keen to regain my freedom, as I thought you might have been.'

'I was, but no matter what the circumstances I never lose my native curiosity. Then when you were sleeping I experimented, making a little heap of the sandy substance that we were working upon and giving it a hearty clout with that little axe that you will recall we used. Well, nothing happened and just as I was settling to sleep the little explosion occurred. I filled an empty vesta box with some of the dust in case we ever got back to London.'

'But, but what does it mean . . . what is it?'

'Oh, I have no idea, Watson, and I don't need to, but I am sure that the scientists at the War Office will have a field day, if they ever get their hands on it.'

I still did not quite understand. 'This then is the fabled secret mineral of Marrafaze. What possible use can it be?'

'Aye, there's the rub, Watson, I can see a very dreadful use for it. In my imagination I see a party of soldiers firing a shell into enemy territory. Although the shell lands with a considerable impact no explosion occurs. But it does erupt, just when the enemy's soldiers, populace even, have gathered around to inspect it. I imagine the fiendish variations that might be effected by the scientists concerning the duration of that lull before the explosion!'

I said nothing and we sat by the fireplace, with our coffee. Holmes selected a pipe, lovingly, revelling in the return to sanity which allowed him to do this. At long last I asked, 'So it was in that sandstone from which the tomb had been hollowed. Do you think it is widespread or just near that place?'

'I imagine, my dear Watson, that it is fairly widespread, and harmless enough in the way it manifests. What it is I don't quite know yet; possibly some combination of sharp sand, volcanic ash and . . . something else that we know not. It may seem bizarre, but whoever uses this upon his fellow human beings may rule the world.'

I watched him light his pipe of Scottish mixture and fill the air around him with an acrid blue smoke. Sherlock Holmes was and is one of the finest men I knew or know. I could not imagine that this man who had worked for so many years so tirelessly for good, to help the oppressed and victims of evil, unleashing this dreadful weapon upon the world.

As usual he read my thoughts. 'You are right, Watson. We can never give this to Mycroft and give our country this sinister advantage. Of course, some day someone will discover it, maybe even during the fruitless search for the fool's gold of Marrafaze. But if we destroy this substance and never tell of it to a living soul at least our consciences will be clear.'

Suddenly he jumped to his feet, laid aside his pipe and went to his bench. I sat where I was, but watching him as he took the vesta box from his robe pocket and opened it, pouring the rest of the substance onto the now slightly charred wooden top. Then he took up the hammer which had not as yet been returned to the grate and gave the little heap a hefty clout. He returned to his chair and relit his pipe with a glowing coal held by fire tongs. We tried to talk of this and that, but could not help but remain alert for the explosion which we knew would come. Of course it did, when we least expected it.

Then Holmes said, 'Be happy now, old friend, for you and I have at least delayed the discovery of the secret weapon of Marrafaze.'

Having been told of the promise that I made, most happily, to Sherlock Holmes never to reveal the existence of the bizarre substance he had discovered, the reader may think it strange that I have written this account. But since that turn-of-the-century adventure no discovery of that devil's sand has been made. You may think that would make it even more important to conceal the fact of its existence. However, no more than a score of years after, a bomb was invented which could be dropped from an aeroplane and would have what was referred to as a 'delayed action'. This was a terrible invention but had no connection whatever with the secret which lies still in an extinct Saharan volcano. The principle involved is, I understand, not connected with the explosive charge but with the mechanism which explodes it.

On a recent visit to see Sherlock Holmes at his cottage in Sussex, where he keeps bees and studies philosophy, I brought up the subject and he agreed that there was no longer need for silence and that the story could be told.

His closing words upon the subject were fascinating. 'My dear Watson, I have mused long upon the subject under discussion for many years. I have changed my mind several times about Mycroft and what his reaction would have been had he known that we had deceived him. If you can call trying to save the world from destruction as deceit. I have recently come to believe that Mycroft did know about it and himself decided to suppress it.'

Was this just an old man trying to think the best of his older brother or did Sherlock base this theory upon his claim that Mycroft had a brain superior even to his own?

I did not ask him!